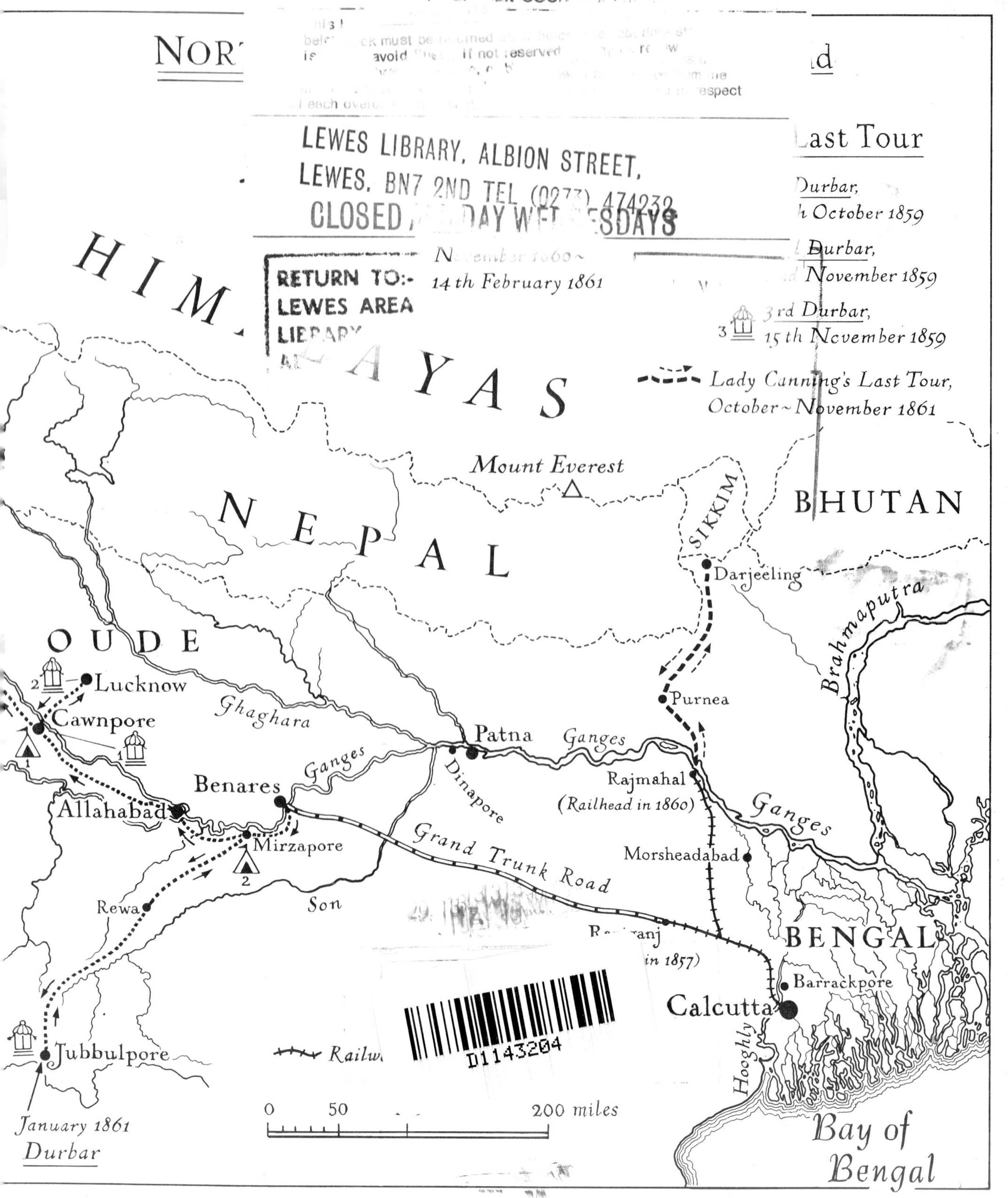

NORT
Last Tour
Durbar,
October 1859
Durbar,
November 1859
3rd Durbar,
15th November 1859
November 1860 ~
14th February 1861
Lady Canning's Last Tour,
October ~ November 1861
HIMALAYAS
Mount Everest
NEPAL
SIKKIM
BHUTAN
Darjeeling
Brahmaputra
OUDE
Lucknow
Cawnpore
Ghaghara
Patna
Ganges
Purnea
Benares
Allahabad
Mirzapore
Dinapore
Rajmahal
(Railhead in 1860)
Grand Trunk Road
Morsheadabad
Rewa
Son
BENGAL
Barrackpore
Calcutta
Hooghly
Jubbulpore
January 1861
Durbar
0 50 200 miles
Bay of Bengal

A Glimpse of the Burning Plain

CHARLOTTE VISCOUNTESS CANNING.
102
F. WINTERHALTER. 1849.

A Glimpse of the Burning Plain

Leaves from the Indian Journals of Charlotte Canning

Charles Allen

Michael Joseph
LONDON

Also by Charles Allen:

Plain Tales from the Raj
Raj: A Scrapbook of British India
Tales from the Dark Continent
A Mountain in Tibet
Tales from the South China Seas
Lives of the Indian Princes
Illustrated Plain Tales from the Raj

First published in Great Britain by Michael Joseph Ltd
44 Bedford Square, London WC1
1986

British Library Cataloguing in Publication Data

Canning, Charlotte, *Countess Canning*
A glimpse of the burning plain: leaves from the
Indian journals of Charlotte Canning.
1. India—Social life and customs
I. Title   II. Allen, Charles
954.03'17   DS421

ISBN 0-7181-2667-X

Typeset and printed in Great Britain by BAS Printers Limited
Over Wallop, Stockbridge, Hampshire
and bound by Hunter & Foulis, Edinburgh

HALF TITLE *Allamanda Cathartica*, a popular garden flower: one of Charlotte Canning's many studies of Indian flowers and shrubs.

FRONTISPIECE Charlotte Canning at thirty-two: a portrait commissioned by Queen Victoria from F. Winterhalter in 1849 (By kind permission of the Earl of Harewood).

Contents

ACKNOWLEDGEMENTS

When Charlotte Canning died in India in November 1861 she left no will. Her drawings, watercolours, letters, journals, photographs and Indian memorabilia were brought back to England by Lord Canning and with his death in June 1862 they passed to his nephew Lord Hubert de Burgh, later Lord Clanricarde. He, in turn, left all his property to his distant kinsman the Sixth Earl of Harewood, who had all Lady Canning's surviving paintings and drawings most handsomely bound in nineteen enormous green leather volumes. Of these eight relate to her six-year exile in India. When the Victorian artist Ruskin spoke so highly of these paintings he was perhaps being no more than polite to his hostess; none are of outstanding merit as works of art, yet taken together they form a unique and fascinating record of a particular experience. They represent one dimension of Charlotte Canning's India, now preserved at Harewood House.

A second dimension took the form of photographs but, alas, of the many thousands known to have been taken by Lady Canning in India or under her auspices – for she was a great patron of photography and a pioneer photographer in her own right – only a handful are known to have survived. A few can be seen in Lady Bayley's memorial album at the India Office Library and Records.

Complementing these visual records are Charlotte Canning's letters and journals, most often written up over two-week periods between mails and intended principally for her mother and sister. However, fifty of these letters were written to Queen Victoria. On her orders they were bound into a special folio, together with a number of other letters relating to Lady Canning's years in India, and preserved in the Royal Archives. The other side of that royal correspondence, in the form of twenty-four letters from Queen Victoria, is to be found – together with what remains of Charlotte Canning's correspondence, journals and memorabilia – in the Canning Papers, which have been deposited by the present Earl of Harewood in the Leeds District Archives, West Yorkshire Archive Service.

By gracious permission of Her Majesty the Queen I have been able to consult and use the letters in the Royal Archives and those amongst the Canning Papers of which the copyright belongs to Her Majesty.

To Lord Harewood I owe a great debt of gratitude both for his kindness in allowing me to draw freely upon the material, literary and pictorial, from the Canning Papers and from Harewood House – and for providing his imprimatur in the form of an entertaining and instructive foreword.

My thanks also to Lord Stanley of Alderley for permission to quote from the letters of his distant kinsman the Hon. John Stanley. In addition, my thanks to

Warren Fenwicke-Clennell, Comptroller of the Harewood Estate, and his staff at Harewood House; to the Hon. Jane Roberts, Curator of the Print Room, and her staff at Windsor Castle; to Jane Langton, Registrar, and Elizabeth Cuthbert, Deputy Registrar, at the Royal Archives, Windsor Castle; to Pat Kattenhorn and Jill Spanner of the Prints and Drawings Room at the India Office Library and Records; to W. J. Connor, District Archivist, and his staff at the Leeds District Archives; Dr. B. M. Wadhwa, Indian Government Liason Officer at Kew, and Miss Sylvia Fitzgerald, Chief Librarian at the Royal Botanic Gardens at Kew, for their help in identifying Lady Canning's drawings of plants and flowers; to Peter Langford at the *Yorkshire Post* for his photography; to Alice Rockwell, for her perfect typing; to Giles Eyre, for his advice; to Graham Ussher, who first drew my attention to the Canning Albums; and, finally, to Alan Haydock, who produced the three-part dramatisation of *A Glimpse of the Burning Plain*, first broadcast on BBC Radio 4 in May 1986.

Lady Canning's paintings are reproduced by kind permission of Lord Harewood.
Additional illustrations are reproduced by kind permission of the following (numbers refer to pages):
HM the Queen – 5, 53, 80–1, 88;
also Lord Harewood – frontispiece, 6, 67, facing 130, 161, 162;
India Office Library and Records – 42, 54, 59, 63, 65, 73, 90, 100, 119, 132, 133, 138, 140, 151, 157, 164;
M. Kaul – 32–3, 72, 87, 92, 114, 124;
Punch – 75, 79;
C. Allen – 150, 167;
Lord Stanley of Alderley – 104;
P. Mills – 82.
Photography at Harewood House and at Leeds District Archives was undertaken by the Yorkshire Post Studios.

FOREWORD

If you grow up in a big house, have parents and several relations with a sense of history, and you start to develop one yourself, you will inevitably at an early age find certain areas of the past illuminated in a way that is vivid if by no means always accurate. This happened to me at Harewood, and I remember causing my parents some surprise when I assured my new governess that a room in the ruined castle, which lies about a mile distant, had been meticulously refurnished for Queen Victoria when she came to stay in the 1830s, which was to put it mildly a gloss on history and true only in the sense that she visited Harewood with her mother. It was the best visitors' bedroom and dressing-room that had been made ready for her! Be that as it may, inextricably involved in my perception of history for almost as long as I can remember were Lady Canning's watercolours, which were to me legendary in that they were constantly referred to by my father but, by me, seldom seen, though half a dozen were framed and hanging on the walls at Harewood.

Canning was a name I had known and revered from infancy. My great-grandmother was granddaughter to George Canning, the Prime Minister, and from her brother his bachelor great-uncle, my father inherited all that remained of the Prime Minister's estate together with what had belonged to his son, Charles, who was Governor-General of India at the time of the Mutiny. The Governor-General's wife, Charlotte Canning, was not only Queen Victoria's lady-in-waiting, but a watercolourist of some distinction to whom her august employer deferred in that area if in no other. They corresponded rather extensively, which was a habit of that pre-telephone period just as sketching served to provide a record of what they saw as did photography for later generations – it is typical as well as logical that the Cannings were early patrons of the art and craft of photography, notably in India.

The Canning Papers, both relating to the Prime Minister and to the Governor-General (like Mountbatten, though in the opposite order, Charles Canning was both Governor-General and Viceroy), I heard constantly mentioned in conversation when I was young. George Canning's reposed in ancient, uniformly bound volumes in the Library at Harewood and my brother and I occasionally carried them from table to shelf when my father perused them; and there were always gaps in the Library when my cousin the historian, Michael Maclagan, borrowed a shelf-full of the Viceroy's papers for his long-planned book about him (*'Clemency' Canning* only appeared well after the 1939–45 war and after an appropriate period for digestion, but it was worth waiting for).

Lady Canning's watercolours were more tangible and apparent to a childish imagination than the Papers. My father when he inherited them had them all mounted and housed in nineteen great leather-bound volumes which reposed in the Library but were taken out quite often after tea for examination and identification. I looked at some of them occasionally but they were more a source of awe in the shelves in their green bindings than of wonder because of what they depicted or how. In any case, they were in store and inaccessible during the war and it was only after I had been to India for the first time in 1958 that my curiosity was again aroused and I discovered how well Lady Canning had done her work of record and comment, and how many of the drawings had transcended those important functions to turn into works of art, enjoyable and a source of delight rather than valuable mainly because of what they recalled.

As a group, they touch on many parts of the world, and I think they show a love of what she saw, wherever she saw it, but particularly a love of India, even though it was India's demands and the exigencies of its climate which were to bring her life and afterwards her husband's to a premature end. Queen Victoria, her indefatigable correspondent, obviously shared that love, in spite of the fact that it was a second-hand emotion since the Queen never experienced the subcontinent. But India's fascination for its visitors is notorious, and Queen Mary for instance never forgot the spell cast on her by the Durbar in 1911 in spite of never visiting India again. As someone who succumbed willingly to India's spell (and lucky in having made quite frequent visits over more that twenty-five years), it is something I find easy to understand and sympathise with.

Possibly Lady Canning would have been satisfied to think of her watercolours lying decently preserved in their volumes in the Library at Harewood or a few of them on our walls. Nonetheless history and conservation, to say nothing of their intrinsic artistic interest, suggest a more positive use, and I am very happy indeed that one of the late twentieth century's conjurors of magic from the British connection with India should have been attracted to them and to the correspondence between my great-great-great aunt by marriage and my great-great grandmother, Queen Victoria, whom she served and who was two years her junior.

Harewood

'A Cloud May Arise'

On a bitterly cold day in early December 1855 the steamer *Caradoc* put out from Marseilles bound for Alexandria. The only passengers on board were the newly appointed Governor-General of India and his wife, Viscount and Lady Canning, together with a few members of their personal staff.

Charles Canning – 'Carlo' to his intimate friends and family – was about to celebrate his forty-third birthday; his wife Charlotte was thirty-eight. To casual observers they must have appeared a singularly privileged and charmed couple, blessed with good looks and good health, titled, successful, comfortable in the exercise of authority. Their portraits confirm this public image. In a chalk sketch dated 1852 by the artist George Richmond we observe the future Governor-General in the very prime of maturity, strong-minded, handsome and self-assured to the point of arrogance. Only his hair, which is beginning to thin on top, lets him down. And a study of Charlotte Canning by E. M. Ward, executed less than a month before their departure for India, portrays her as the very model of Victorian femininity, as a woman of mild disposition with an intelligent, oval face just teetering on the verge of plumpness. In this case, it is the heavy eyebrows and too firm chin which suggest that the lady is not quite what the artist wants her to be.

The Cannings had been married for twenty years and were childless. They came from Britain's minor aristocracy, of largely Scottish ancestry, both with fathers who had involved themselves in political affairs, one as a statesman, the other as a diplomat. George Canning had been a distinguished Foreign Minister who had died in office as Prime Minister in 1827. His widow had been created a viscountess and with her death in 1838 the title passed to Charles. Charlotte Canning's father, Sir Charles Stuart, had been elevated to the peerage in 1828 after a decade of service in Paris as British Ambassador, taking the title of Lord Stuart de Rothesay. Her mother was a daughter of the Fourth Earl of Hardwicke, which was how Charlotte and her younger sister Louisa came to spend much of their early childhood on one of the Hardwicke estates, Tyttenhanger Park near St Albans. In later years an extraordinary Gothic pile named Highcliffe Castle, built by their father on a crumbling clifftop overlooking Christchurch Bay on the Hampshire coast, became their family home.

Pretty, high-spirited, intelligent and accomplished – with an obvious talent for drawing and painting – 'Char' Stuart created a very favourable impression when she came out into London society in the summer of 1834. One year earlier Charles Canning had come down from Oxford with a first-class honours degree in classics and an assured future in English political life. But although 'singularly handsome and a great gentleman in character and demeanour', his reserve won him few friends outside a close circle of intimates. 'A proud, reserved and sensitive man,' was how one of his Private Secretaries in later years was to describe him, 'for whom one felt the utmost respect, but perhaps not much deep affection, his natural demeanour being too cold to admit of this. He had however a warm heart.' The girl who first stirred this 'warm heart' of his was seventeen-year-old Charlotte Stuart de Rothesay. They fell in love and, despite opposition from Lord Stuart de Rothesay, determined to marry. According to James Bruce, who had been at Eton with Canning and then at Christ Church, Oxford (and who, as Lord Elgin, would later succeed him as Viceroy of India), 'their affection was so true and deep that at last consent was given and from that same year Lord C. was so devoted to her that he could not bear her out of his sight'. The wedding took place at St Martin's-in-the-Fields in September 1835 and after a few days spent at Lady Stuart's house in Richmond the newlyweds moved on to Highcliffe for the rest of their honeymoon.

It took some time for Charles Canning to find his feet in politics. He won a seat in the House of Commons in 1836 but within six months the sudden death of his mother saw him elevated to the House of Lords. Finding it impossible over the next three years to play any worthwhile role on the opposition benches, he spent much of his time – together with his wife – staying with friends and relatives in the country and in making two extended sea voyages through the Mediterranean. Then in 1841 Sir Robert Peel brought Canning into the Foreign Office as Under-Secretary and for the next five years he was deeply involved in government affairs. Charlotte Canning's life style also changed dramatically. In June 1842 she received a letter from the Queen asking her to take up a royal appointment that was about to become vacant, that of Lady of the Bedchamber. Encouraged by her husband, she accepted what was to all intents a royal command.

OPPOSITE Viscountess Canning, 1855, from a preparatory study by E. M. Ward for his oil-painting, 'The Installation of Emperor Napoleon III as a Knight of the Garter' (By gracious permission of Her Majesty the Queen).

As Lady of the Bedchamber Charlotte was required to attend the Queen – to 'wait' upon her, in court language – at various times during the year for periods that varied from a fortnight to more than a month. Even though the duties were never very onerous and the office carried considerable prestige, complete self-effacement and compliance to the Queen's wishes was expected. However, if Lady Canning had any doubts or objections she never made them known, taking up her role with exemplary zeal and characteristic modesty.

The first opportunity for the Queen to get to know her new Lady of the Bedchamber was over Christmas at Windsor Castle in 1842. After a walk together in the park on the afternoon of 20 December, Queen Victoria noted in her journal that Lady Canning was 'a remarkably nice person, so quiet, unaffected and gentle and so ready to do anything'. On that same day Charlotte wrote to her mother that she found the Queen 'very kind and pleasant and I do not at all dislike being here. Canning paid me a visit of four days and I suppose will be asked again at Christmas.' Nevertheless, she had no illusions over her function, noting in the same letter that 'this week nearly all my fellow servants change which I am sorry for – for I had got so used to the present set'.

So began a duty that was to continue for thirteen years, during which time a strong bond of affection and mutual respect was built up between Queen and subject, as their letters and journals confirm. Queen Victoria, two years younger than 'Char' Canning, trusted her as a very sensible and discreet confidante; while the latter, for her part, enjoyed the confidence placed in her as well as the company of this most warm-hearted of British monarchs.

What strains their enforced separation for several months every year may have placed on the Cannings' marriage is a matter for conjecture. What is beyond dispute is that at some point in the late 1840s Charles Canning became deeply involved with another woman and remained so for some years, a shadowy relationship that was common knowledge among his contemporaries. In November 1849 the matter threatened to become a public scandal after Canning peppered a member of the royal household with birdshot during a Windsor shoot. He fainted, apparently fearing that he had hit the young Prince of Wales, but it was whispered about that his behaviour was the result of a row with his mistress which he had feared might come to the notice of the Queen. The only recorded comment on the estrangement of husband and wife comes from Canning's old school friend James Bruce, who considered it 'one of the saddest instances he had ever known of a true love marriage turning out unhappily'. All had been well when Bruce

OPPOSITE Viscount Canning, 1852, from a chalk drawing by George Richmond (By kind permission of the Earl of Harewood).

had left to take up the appointment of Governor-General of Canada in 1846: 'I was absent for some years and when I returned all that was sadly changed and another woman's affections had brought great unhappiness in their house.' Charlotte Canning bore this loss of her husband's affections with fortitude and apparently without bitterness. Not a word or indication of her own distress was ever spoken or written.

In 1853 Canning was offered the position of Postmaster-General in Lord Aberdeen's new government. Two years later the question of selecting a successor to Lord Dalhousie in India came up and various names were canvassed. The final choice of Charles Canning was entirely unexpected and the Queen, who had not been consulted, was furious. 'She takes a deep and natural interest in the welfare of her Indian Empire, and must consider the selection of the fittest person for the post of Governor-General as of paramount importance', she wrote indignantly to the President of the Board of Control. 'She had frequently discussed this point with Lord Palmerston, but the name of Lord Canning never occurred among the candidates alluded to. The Queen is even now quite ignorant as to the reasons and motives which led to his selection in preference to those other names, and Mr V. Smith will see at once that, were the Queen inclined to object to it, she could not *now* do so without inflicting a deep, personal injury on a public man, for whose personal qualities and talents the Queen has a high regard.'

Gossip had it that the appointment had been engineered by one of Charles Canning's most influential friends, Lord Lansdowne, in order to get him away from the spell of his *inamorata*. Whatever the motives, the prospect of the appointment certainly did not appeal to Charlotte Canning. 'There are really no reasons against accepting but one's own feelings and dislikes', she confided to her sister Louisa, now Marchioness of Waterford and living in Ireland. 'But I will not take any part in the decision, only be ready to follow like a dog. If it was only for one year I should delight in it, but five is terribly long.' On 16 June she broke the news to her mother that Lord Canning had accepted and that they would be leaving for India before the end of the year: 'Now we must try and think it is still a good while before the moment arrives. I believe we must not talk about it yet, and indeed it feels a respite to keep it quiet as long as possible.'

For the rest of the summer and the autumn Lady Canning spent as much time as she could with her family, her sister joining her from Ireland. One last spell in waiting was passed at Balmoral before the time came for Charlotte and the two maids, West and Rain, who were to accompany her, to prepare for departure.

Charles Canning was also busily employed, handing over the reins of office of his old post and building up as much knowledge as he could of the new one. On 1 August he had taken the oath of office at the Indian Office in Leadenhall Street and that same evening had spoken at a banquet given in his honour by the Court of Directors of the East India Company. His speech had contained the customary indications as to the policies that his administration would endeavour to pursue, but it had closed on a note of warning that was soon to acquire the status of a prophecy:

> I wish for a peaceful time of office, but I cannot forget that in our Indian Empire the greatest of all blessings depends upon a greater variety of chances and a more precarious tenure than in any other quarter of the globe. We must not forget that in the sky of India, serene as it is, a cloud may arise, at first no bigger than a man's hand, but which growing bigger and bigger, may at last threaten to overwhelm us with ruin.

On 22 November the Cannings called formally on the Queen and Prince Albert at Windsor and made their farewells. 'After our breakfast we took leave of the dear Cannings, with great regret', noted Queen Victoria in her journal. 'They start on the 26th.'

CHAPTER I

'How Like a Dream'

Until the opening of the Suez Canal in 1869 brought India five thousand miles closer to England, voyages by what was known as the 'long sea' route to the subcontinent were protracted affairs occupying many months. However, by taking two overland short cuts it was possible to knock two or even three months off the journey time, and this was the method chosen by the Cannings. The first overland leg was across France by train to Marseilles, where the *Caradoc* was waiting to be boarded. After several uncomfortable days of rough seas, during which Char Canning was the only passenger to 'retain full possession of appetite and stomach', the skies cleared and they arrived in Alexandria in warm sunshine – to be received in oriental splendour by representatives of the Egyptian ruler, Ismail Pasha.

At the time of their leave-taking at Windsor Queen Victoria had made a point of asking Charlotte to write to her, and so on 19 December she sat down to pen the first of a series of lively and often amusing letters to the Queen:

> Madam,
> As your Majesty so kindly expressed a wish to hear from me I venture to write, for tho' this is but a very early stage in our long journey we have seen and done so much that I could easily believe we had been away 3 months rather than 3 weeks. Our voyage was most agreeable (tho' perhaps others liked it less than I) as we had very strong fair wind and rough seas to Malta – the comfort of being in the Caradoc instead of a crowded passenger vessel is not to be described. After Malta each day was more & more beautiful, and within 8 days of leaving Marseilles we were at Alexandria, enjoying the hot sun.
>
> I cannot tell your Majesty how much civility & what honours have been paid to us by the Pasha. From the moment we were landed at Alexandria in his barge we have been provided with everything it is possible to wish for. The palace we were lodged in had been quite furnished & so completely did they wish to suit

OPPOSITE The Great Temple of Karnac at Thebes, first explored by moonlight on Christmas night 1855 and revisited next morning: 'We were there at 7 in the morning & stayed the whole day, resting & having meals in the shadow of the temple.'

their preparations to their notion of European habits that we found in each room a supply of new combs and brushes, and even tooth brushes and tooth powder.

Although the Cannings had previously travelled as far east as Constantinople, nothing from their earlier journeys had prepared them for the impact of Alexandria and Egypt:

> The first impression of the real East has an indescribable effect. Such extraordinary figures in various dresses, veiled women, strings of camels, and the buildings and strange southern vegetation make one feel in a dream. I long to draw and so regret being unable to sketch figures when everyone is so picturesque. The land is like the richest gardens, and the view ranges over crops of rice, wheat, cotton and sugar cane, and wretched mud villages with their palm trees raised on mounds just high enough to escape the innundation.
>
> The Pasha ordered that we should have the advantage of the new railway as far as Cairo. The greatest work is where it crosses the Damietta branch [of the Nile] on the top of Stevenson's tubular bridge. We are lodged here [in Cairo] in a Palace belonging to Ismail Pasha, Said Ibrahim, who is said to have laid out £150,000 in its decorations. It is a mile from the town & its garden opens upon the Nile, I really believe, near the spot where Moses was found. I really cannot describe the gorgeous and enormous rooms — the centre salon is 155 ft. by 60 ft. and furnished with all the gold papers & damask & ormulu & clocks & lustres that Paris could supply as suitable to Egyptian taste. We found it difficult to prevent the servant from lighting 700 candles in one room the first night – with all this luxe we rather look forward to embarking on the steamer to take

OPPOSITE ABOVE The temple at Philae. 'That lovely island of temples & palm trees, above the first cataract', was how Charlotte described it to Queen Victoria. BELOW Edfou, above Thebes, 27 December 1855.

The rooftops of Alexandria, sketched from Baghos Bey's Palace, 13 December 1855. 'We have been received with the greatest honour here,' wrote Charlotte in her journal, 'and are quite astonished at the Pasha's munificence – his barge sent for us, & a palace prepared, furnished, filled with servants, & supplying sumptuous meals.'

us up to the first Cataract, for this is like a gorgeous prison, and we are behind latticed windows shutting out all view, for the harem often stays here! A number of black slaves peculiarly employed to wait upon these ladies are constantly about, & whenever we move 4 men in the Egyptian dress with silver sticks go before us shaking them, & ride before the carriage.

While Lord Canning called formally on the ruler to pay his respects, Char made a more informal call on his wife, accompanied by two English ladies whose husbands were directing the building of the new railway:

We were received first at the door by the blacks: then about 20 Circassian slave girls, like the chorus of an opera, scampered down the garden & threw themselves round us & handed us along lifting one partly under the arm & marched us through courts and halls up to a great gallery at the end of which Madame Said Pasha sat. She came forward to receive me & led me to another room to sit by her on her cushions, & then sweetmeats & an assortment of pipes with magnificent amber mouth pieces covered with jewels. I succeeded in smoking a few whiffs of each pipe & I really think it was received in good spirit. The great lady is very handsome, and has such a gentle charming expression that one feels she is too good for her fate. She is about 26 years old & has no child. She is taller than me & more like Lady Conyngham [mistress of George IV] than anyone I can think of – but fairer. She was a Circassian adopted by Mehemet Ali's daughter, who married her at 15 to her brother. This elder sister of the Pasha sent for us and received us with extraordinary dignity, such as one would not have imagined in a poor sick lady crouched up on her bed on a pile of cushions. Of all Mehemet Ali's children she is said to have resembled him most in talent, & was mixed

'Like a gorgeous prison'; the view from Ismael Pasha's Palace, Cairo, December 1855.

The Nile at Minieh, 22 December 1855: 'I am convinced that, with leisure, the boats are the really enjoyable way of seeing Egypt.'

> up all her life in political intrigue & very cruel & wicked in other respects. She seems so ill now that they hardly expect her to recover.

Signing herself with due formality as 'Your Majesty's dutiful humble servant, C. Canning', Char ended this first letter with the news that they were setting off up the Nile that evening. This was to be their last real holiday before Lord Canning immersed himself in his gubernatorial duties: a leisurely three-week excursion by river steamer that would take them five hundred miles south as far as the First Cataract at Aswan.

For the only time on their journey Char Canning was able to indulge her artistic inclinations to the full, first at the ancient ruins of Memphis, which they toured in the company of 'janissaries and old men with silver sticks & bells, & pipe-bearers, & coffee-bearers, who go with us wherever we go, some on donkeys, some

on horseback – an endless cavalcade'. On Christmas Day they were moored alongside the temple of Dendara. Clambering through its inner chambers, they found themselves surrounded by bats that 'hung like branches of grapes from the roof and came flopping about our heads to the light of the candle each person carried. We walked in bat-guano, and breathed a double distilled perfume of bat, till it was impossible to stand it any longer: especially when I began to think I was treading on the killed and wounded we had disturbed and knocked down.'

That night after dinner they landed to explore the temple complex at Karnak where, as Charlotte noted later in her journal:

> the moonlight through the palm trees delighted me most of all, then an avenue of sphinxes and the great pylon. There we left our donkeys and got rid of most of our train, and went round enormous ruins to the great temple. This is really like a work of giants – a grove of gigantic columns, & piles of stones & obelisks, one 92 feet high, and courts with pillars round them, & more & more of the great pylons, all magnified even, in the bright moonlight.

Rising early next morning Char returned with her easel and her watercolours and spent the whole day sketching and painting, 'with the bluest of skies and all the ruins of a rich yellow colour'.

After visiting the island temple of Philae, just above the cataracts, the Cannings returned to Cairo – where there was one final excursion to be made before they continued on their way to India. 'I think of all we saw the Pyramids "impress" one most', Charlotte informed the Queen in her second letter. 'We dived down the sloping narrow passages & climbed up to the centre chamber, but I must own we did not succeed in mounting to the top of the outside.' But, as Char explained in detail to her mother, this was telling only half the story:

> I arrived with the full intention of going up, then the scramble rather alarmed me. But as C. told me to do as I pleased I started & was helped up charmingly by the Arabs for a little distance, perhaps 100 ft. Then arrived C. at the same resting place, he had a great dread of looking down from a height & he thought the sight of me being dragged up the stones over his head so very horrid & the prospect of going down so much worse, that I actually offered to turn back if he pleased, & he joyfully accepted. I minded it so very little & found the clever way the Arabs had of lowering me down so very easy, that I have never ceased regretting that we did not persevere.

OPPOSITE Dendera, 25 December 1855: 'The inner chambers of the temples were quite dark, & we crept through a hole into a secret passage with very perfect sculptures, & were busy examining them till literally driven out by the cloud of bats.'

The next stage of their journey was a race in horse-drawn carriages across the desert to Suez over a route 'marked with the skeletons of dead camels', so many that the two maids gave up counting when they had reached a figure of 162 in four hours. Waiting offshore at Suez was an East India Company steam frigate, whose captain received them on board with great ceremony: 'We found the Feroze a steam frigate larger even than your Majesty's former yacht and comfortably fitted up & adapted for a hot climate. It was a foretaste of India to see sepoy marines, half the crew black, servants in white muslin & gold & turbans & sashes, to hear of tiffin instead of luncheon, to be fanned all dinner time, & many other rich peculiarities in their details.'

Eight days of 'agreeably monotonous' sailing brought the Cannings to Aden – whose 'cinder-like mountains of volcanic formation are so bare & so fantastic in shape that they reminded me of nothing but Mr Nasmyth's Ideal Views of the Moon' – and another eight took them to Bombay. 'Here we are! Really in India! It feels very like a dream!' wrote Charlotte enthusiastically in her journal on 29 January 1856:

Aden and the screened verandah of the Governor's house: 'The mountains are enormously high & nearly perpendicular, & the peaks of fantastic shape – very black & red & yellow, like burnt out cinders, & as full of holes. The Governor's house is on the point, on a spot catching every breath of wind. It has neither walls nor windows, & is literally a cage of trellised reeds, with here & there a mat hung up to intercept the view.'

> We steamed in rather slowly yesterday afternoon, with the bay unfolding before us like a panorama, a beautiful coast, with a great expanse of high odd-shaped hills, and a good deal of green at the foot: some islands, and the town itself on one of them – the greenest. It had an air de fête in the bright sunset sky, many sailing boats about, and the ships dressed with flags, and yards manned and saluting. The instant we anchored, Lord Elphinstone [Governor of Bombay Presidency 1853–8] came on board, and Sir H. Leake, who is at the head of the Indian navy, and we went ashore in their barge. The twilight is very short here, and it was all but dark when we arrived at the landing place. Lord Dalhousie had ordered that all the troops should be out, and that we should be received in state, so it was a very grand affair. The people in authority received us, and off we drove in a barouche & four, with a turbanned postillion & an escort of lancers, & the road was lined with soldiers. Crowds and crowds of natives in their white dresses, Parsees and all sorts of picturesque people, were outside and bands playing etc. The native town looked most picturesque – all open shops and verandahs, and the strangest figures scattered about and lighted up.

Bombay Island in 1856 was still innocent of the industrialisation that was to transform it into India's main generator of wealth before the end of the century. 'Bombay is a most beautiful country with every variety of hill & rock & wood & water', Charlotte informed the Queen. 'I who so much delight in plants thoroughly appreciate the beauty of the tropical vegetation.' The Cannings had been lodged at Government House at Parel, then totally surrounded by open countryside:

> From my window I see groves and groves of cocoa [sic] and palm overtopping round-headed trees; then burnt-up ground; mango-trees in flower exactly like Spanish chestnuts; tamarinds in the style of acacias, but much thicker; peepul-trees, higher a good deal than the rest, with trembling leaves – very green, and pinkish stems, like white poplar; a teak tree, with large leaves and sort of bunches of berries. Little green parrots fly about, and settle in the tamarind tree, looking like green peas, and hawks and odd crows – grey and black – flutter about. Very slightly clothed peasants fill up the picture, and sometimes beautifully draped figures in white.

Government House itself was no less exotic, being an old Portuguese seminary that had been converted into a country mansion where 'everything is arranged for coolness', with 'doors in all directions, made like Venetian blinds, and broad verandahs all round the rooms'. Meals were taken on 'a verandah entirely draped with white muslin, with those beautifully dressed servants to wait, and strange fruits on the table, and strange flowers, and a very good band of music outside'. In her bedroom 'a tent of net, with a weight round the edge, defends my bed from mosquitos, and there is room for chairs and little tables within'. Other curious fixtures were the enormous tubs and baths of water to be found in every room:

'People go into them after exercise, doing exactly what we should think the most dangerous thing possible. In the same way, iced water is drunk all day long.'

Even though another six weeks or so remained of what was termed the Cold Weather, Char found the days too warm for comfort. She observed that this sustained heat seemed to make people 'very quiet, and gentle and low, for I had rather a feeling as if I was brusque and noisy, so very piano is the tone. Nobody looks sunburnt – boiled to rags rather than roasted, is certainly the effect of the climate.' Three days after their arrival she noted wryly in her journal that 'I suppose I shall never feel as fresh again as I was, just off my sea-voyage.'

A series of official engagements and excursions had been arranged for the Cannings' eight days in Bombay. On the third day the new Governor-General met some of the city's leading citizens at a formal levée and durbar at the Town Hall, one ceremony being for the Europeans, the other for the Indians. His wife watched the proceedings from a balcony. 'Each person after making his salam sits down', began her description of the scene to the Queen. 'A little rose water is sprinkled on him with a spoon. A bit of Pawn [*paan*], which is a composition of lime &

The Governor's Villa, Parel, Bombay. 'I am quite charmed with it,' wrote Charlotte in her journal on 29 January 1856. 'Everything is arranged for coolness, & it seems to answer, for I never felt a pleasenter atmosphere. Last night, with all its arches & verandahs lighted up, & rows of servants in scarlet & gold dresses or in white, it looked like a opera scene'.

betel nut fastened up in gold leaf, is given to him to chew & a little bunch of flowers & after a little time leave is given to the company to disperse.' The next day they were up at four to be first driven in carriages and then carried in sedan chairs out to a hillside at Salsette honeycombed with ancient Buddhist caves. Char found the style of their outing 'curiously Indian. If we had come to live a fortnight in these caves, there could not have been more elaborate preparations – carpets, furniture, crockery, looking-glasses, and an enormous bath!, a dressing-room for each of us, batterie de cuisine, plate, linen, and glass: and, in going round, I found all this luxury was not only for me and C., but really the same for every A.D.C.'

Over the next few days other visits were made to every corner of the island and to various institutions. What Charlotte least enjoyed was her attendance at church on Sunday in a building festooned with 'odious punkahs', oblong fans 'painted in stone-coloured panels and a solid flap appended at the bottom', that were pulled by ropes operated by hidden punkah-wallahs outside the church:

> It was a cool fine pleasant day & the church large & airy, pews of rails, & everyone in a separate chair. The fuss of punkahs was wholly unnecessary, but there they were going like mad! I shall never forget the effect! Imagine a bad dream, in which all the gallery front of a large London church should detach and swing across to meet their opposite neighbours, all going backwards and forwards at a great pace and no noise. At first, it was very difficult not to laugh, and then not to cry, the effect was so irritating, and one would have given anything to entreat them to stop. They pass within a few feet of one's head, and leave a sort of mesmerising effect that one feels inside one's head. To shut one's eyes is the only relief.

What was undoubtedly the most satisfying engagement from Lady Canning's point of view was spent giving out prizes at one of Bombay's pioneering girls' schools. The subject of women's education was something that both she and Queen Victoria took very seriously and over the next few years Char was to devote much of her time and energy to its promotion:

> The natives appreciate education very much & of late a great change of opinion has come upon them with respect to the education of girls. Their schools lately established now contain upward of 700! & a distribution of prizes to these little creatures was one of the most curious sights we have seen. Some were Parsees, others Hindoos, all covered with finery, gold & jewels, their brown skins peeping thro' chains & necklaces, and the pretty little faces usually disfigured by nose rings. They delight in learning but are taken away to be married when quite children & I am not sure that they learn a great deal that is useful, but this beginning must lead to a great change in their condition. The boys of the schools &

> colleges learn English & speak it well [but] there is a strong prejudice against allowing the girls to learn a word of it.

From Bombay the Cannings proceeded in their steam frigate to Ceylon and then up the Coromandel Coast to Madras. As the *Feroze* approached Madras Roads on the night of 13 February, making good speed with a following wind, Char was awoken by 'a great bump and a lurch' that she took to be a collision: 'I thought we were into the Calcutta steamer; but no, it was a rock. A second bump, and we were off again and all right. It was very absurd to see all the cabin doors open, and the white figures darting about. I did not go on deck, for I knew so well it would bore people, who mentally would say, "Those women are always in the way"; but very soon C. came down to tell me the news, and it was that we were rather too near the shore, and Captain Rennie, himself on the paddle-box and looking out, chanced to touch the fag-end of the Tripalore rocks.' Her two English maids were tested on this occasion: 'West fluttered about in her night-shift, with "Oh dear, Oh dear me!" in a terrible state, and yet was so tractable as to be entirely comforted and quieted at my merely saying, "It is nothing at all: you must not be a goose," and patting her to quiet her. Rain never said a word, but deliberately lighted her candle, and then came to say, "Your dark dressing-gown's out, my lady".'

Viewed from the sea Madras, with its long sandy beach, looked like 'a scrap of Brighton'. Every passenger had to be conveyed in small local craft over the breakers to the shore, where 'a chair is put at the edge of the boat, into which you sit, and are triumphantly carried away – looking very ridiculous'. Here the Cannings were looked after by Lord Harris, Governor of Madras Presidency and an old school friend of Charles Canning's, who introduced them to every senior civil and military officer in the region by 'having 34 people to dinner every day for more than a week'. They were taken out to inspect the new railway line, reaching fifty miles into the interior of the subcontinent, opened flower shows and visited schools – including a mission school where Lady Canning found 'the phraseology and manners of some of the missionaries most disagreeable. All the boys seemed to have religious knowledge and doctrine at their finger-ends, and answered in the very unconstrained manner of the missionaries, using their very words: and yet one knew they did not pretend to believe or think what they said.' Even if she did not yet realise it, Char Canning's unease was well-founded. What was happening at the Free Kirk Mission School at Madras was part of a much larger pattern of events whose consequences would soon become all too apparent.

Charlotte also found the manners and life styles of her compatriots in Madras more than a little absurd:

It is not extraordinary that the sort of English people who have lived all their lives in India are not happy when they go home to England again. They must feel so fallen in position – living in Maida Hill or Cheltenham, instead of in these enormous houses with great rooms twenty feet high, brilliantly lighted, with servants in crowds, and treated with a sort of pomp and circumstance unknown to anybody in England. They have very smart equipages – carriages for the day-time, with Venetian blinds all round, and barouches for evening. Their servants, in white, have pretty flat turbans, and sashes of the colour of their master. Two runners or Saises, with fly-flappers of horse-hair, keep up with whatever pace the carriage goes, and strange to say never look out of breath. Every horse has a servant of his own and a grass-cutter. Dogs have each their own servant. We saw a newly-arrived dog in his stall, provided with a night-light, besides his other comforts and his valet de chambre.

These were not the sort of observations that could be confided to one's monarch. They went into Char's journal and were intended for her mother's and suitor's eyes alone. As yet, Lady Canning's relations with the Queen were friendly but hardly intimate – and her first letters to Queen Victoria from India were formal and even a little awkward in manner. In Madras she chose to write at some length on the safe subject of Indian women and children:

The women are most graceful in their long draperies in bold like Greek statues & of brilliant heavy colours and narrow bright borders, green, red, orange, crimson being the usual colours. The little children naked & like bronze cling to their mothers & ride astride on their hips in a very peculiar manner. I am so very sorry to be utterly unable to draw these picturesque figures. Photography is making good progress in India & I hope soon to send some specimens to your Majesty. How I wish that your Majesty could see the most interesting part of your dominions & I often think how much His Royal Highness would delight in the study of these races of people and their curious habits and in the symptoms of improvement working in them.

This second letter to the Queen, sent from Madras in late February, crossed with Queen Victoria's enthusiastic reply to the first:

Windsor Castle,
January 25th 1856

Dearest Lady Canning,
Your first very interesting letter of the 19th Dec. from Cairo has given me the greatest pleasure, & I thank you very much for it. How very wonderful all those oriental luxuries & customs must be, & how like a dream it must all appear to European eyes! If it was not for the heat and the insects how much I should like to see India . . .

CHAPTER II

'I Never Knew What Idleness Was Before'

At exactly half past five in the afternoon on 29 February 1856 the barge carrying India's fourteenth Governor-General arrived opposite Chandpal Ghat on the corner of Calcutta's central *maidan*. Salutes were fired from the nearby ramparts of Fort William, flags fluttered from the rigging of the many naval vessels and merchantmen at anchor in the Hooghly, and British and Indian troops lined the short route that led up Esplanade Row to Government House. Much to her indignation, however, Charlotte Canning found herself a spectator at her husband's ceremonial arrival rather than an active participant. Their leisurely journey up the Hooghly channel of the Ganges to the East India Company's administrative headquarters had been punctuated by a series of directives from the outgoing Governor-General, Lord Dalhousie, setting out exactly what to expect and what was required of them upon their arrival. The last of these had informed them that according to precedent the new Governor-General should land unaccompanied:

> C. of course agreed to whatever was proposed, but I don't think he admired the arrangement much more than I did, and it was not a pleasant addition to such an affair to have to make my public entry by myself. I did not feel at all good-humoured about it, I own. I had my choice whether to land before or after C., so I pocketed my grievance, and settled to land first, and see him arrive, instead of following after, quite privately, when the crowd had dispersed, and all his show was at an end. I was sent off in a boat, with one of Lord Dalhousie's aides-de-camp. I walked through an avenue of triumphal arches, with flags and hundreds of spectators on each side, up a road of red cloth to our own little barouche, which looked surprised at itself, with four horses and Eastern postillions in dresses of red, black, and gold.

Entering the grounds of Government House by a side entrance, Lady Canning was met by Lord Dalhousie's daughter, Lady Susan, whose mother had died three years earlier in particularly tragic circumstances. It was the Marchioness of Dalhousie whom Char had succeeded as Lady-in-Waiting to Queen Victoria. She and Lord Dalhousie had come out to India in 1848, leaving their children behind in England. Five years later she had been sent home an invalid, dying within sight of land as her ship sailed up the Bristol Channel. Her place as hostess at Government House had been filled by her eldest daughter, Susan, whom Char found to be full of 'aplomb and character and as merry as possible, but so sorry to go away'.

Her father appeared to be equally sad to be leaving, but it was also obvious that he was 'shattered in health' and only able to walk with the aid of a crutch. As soon as the swearing-in ceremony that followed immediately upon Lord Canning's arrival at Government House was over, Char had an opportunity to observe the change that eight years in India had wrought in him: 'Lord Dalhousie came into the drawing room, where I went and sat with him, and – oh how sad to see the change in him, and he is but forty-three! Nothing could be more cheerful and agreeable than I found him, and yet, poor man, how he seemed to be suffering.'

In his eight years as Governor-General Dalhousie had been instrumental in bringing about many far-reaching changes to the political landscape of the Indian subcontinent. Railway tracks, steamer services and telegraph lines had begun to draw distant places together in a way that had never been possible before, while the East India Company's *raj* or rule had been extended by thousands of square miles. Two wars had added the Punjab and Lower Burma to what was now being termed the Indian Empire, a number of princely states whose rulers had died without legitimate heirs had been absorbed and even the once-powerful Kingdom of Oude, with its capital at Lucknow, was in the final stages of annexation, its Nawab having been declared unfit to rule. In the interests of good government and with the best of intentions India was being bullied into the nineteeth century – and all but the most sceptical regarded the future with confidence. Lady Canning certainly had no doubts. 'All has become prosperous and quiet', she assured the Queen in a letter written a week after their arrival. 'So many great works are in hand that I trust we have much to look forward to cheerfully.'

Despite the reassuring tone of her letter – in which she went on to describe her immediate surroundings as having 'a very English appearance, like the flat part of Hyde Park & the high houses to the north side' – Char's first impressions of Calcutta were anything but favourable. 'This is a hopelessly difficult house to manage', she confided in her journal, 'and – oh, there are deficiencies in Calcutta which no one ever told me of, but which are enough to deter any one from ever coming voluntarily to live here.' As soon as the Dalhousies had departed she took stock of her situation: 'The reality of our being established here for five years comes now vividly before me, and at last I begin to feel we are not on a tour! C. is very full of work, and I of idleness, but on Monday I shall begin to arrange the house.'

Modelled on Kedlestone Hall in Derbyshire but built of brick covered with a veneer of plaster rather than stone, Government House was a grandiose three-storeyed building designed to impress rather than provide homely comfort. However, it was admirably suited to make the most of even the slightest puff of wind, being x-shaped with four wings linked to a central core by curving three-tiered galleries. The Cannings occupied the first and second floors of the south-west wing, facing out across the broad green expanse of the *Maidan*. Rather in the manner of an Indian potentate, the Governor-General had his own quarters on the first floor, surrounded by his aides-de-camp and Private Secretary, while Lady Canning occupied the rooms above: 'I live on the second floor, over C., and they have built a winding staircase from his sitting-room to mine. A sitting-room au second makes one feel like recovering from a long illness.' This sitting-room led out on to a long balcony under a colonnade 'inhabited by numberless screeching birds'. During their first inspection of the house Char had been on the point of complaining about the noise 'when C. told me to come and look and I found there were about fifteen of the brightest, sleekest green parroquets [the roseringed parakeet or *tota*], with pink rings round their throats. They made their nests in the capitals of the pillars and corners of the beams; and a number of other odd kinds congregate there too, and are so pretty that one must tolerate their noise.'

As well as their own sitting-rooms there was a reception room on the second floor at the rear of an enormous ballroom that Char at once took upon herself to transform into 'the most civilised room in India'. Although 'newly furnished and very handsomely done in red damask chairs', it was essentially a long gallery providing access to the two south-facing wings of the house and with no less than nine doors, 'of which all but one are always open'. Defying Anglo-Indian custom, which decreed that 'no chairs or sofas will ever be sat upon unless they are under the influence of the line of punkahs along the centre', she set about transforming the room to reflect her own tastes, rearranging the furniture and covering everything in her favourite light chintzes. With the arrival of a number of portraits of the royal family, despatched by the Queen, the transformation of the gallery into a comfortable drawing-room that was 'pretty and cool and English' was complete.

Other long-established Anglo-Indian conventions were not so easy to breach, however. The kitchens were situated at a distance not less than 150 yards from the dining-room, with 'no means of keeping the soufflés from collapsing on the way', and there was not a single water closet to be found in the whole of Calcutta,

let alone Government House. The excuse was that there was 'no fall for drainage' in the flat alluvial plain upon which the city stood, but the plain fact was that it was easier to rely upon the army of untouchables who serviced the earth closets and commodes.

Even to those used to the proximity of servants in large numbers, as the Cannings undoubtedly were, their constant attendance was another aspect of Indian life that needed getting used to, as Charlotte admitted in her journal:

> There is rather less bother than I expected in the way of a tail of servants following me about. I am not sure that I do not regret creaking footmen. These gliding people come & stand by one, & will wait an hour with their eye fixed on one, & their hands joined as if to say their prayers, if you do not see them – & one is quite startled to find them patiently waiting when one looks round. I have

Fragments of daily life in Government House, Calcutta, from Lady Canning's sketch-book. Of the adjutant birds Charlotte wrote, 'the balustrades are garnished with rows of enormous cranes, called adjutants, hideous birds who congregate in the rains'.

Servants Government House (Summer Dress)

Parroquets in the verandah

Servants Government House (Winter Dress)

Adjutants top of Government House in the rains

Parroquets

> insisted on having my bed made & room swept by a woman, & one has been got, but she is quite of a low caste, and I have not got an ayah, and doubt if I shall want one. The showing up of visitors, & taking them away, & all that sort of footman's work, is entirely done by aides-de-camp, which is a horrid bore. I have such scruples at giving them so many journeys up & down, & it *is* indeed far pleasanter to have a creaking footman in livery.

Nor were Lady Canning's scruples confined to the employment of her husband's ADCs as footmen. She worried about the punkah-pullers who worked the overhead fans and for some weeks into the Hot Weather, now beginning to make itself felt with ever-increasing ferocity as March gave way to April, held out against employing a punkah-wallah at night. 'I doubt if I shall ever have it pulled at night', she assured herself on 11 March. 'The evenings really are not very hot, the rooms are so very airy & the punkahs go incessantly. I have actually submitted now & then to one in my room, & it certainly *is* pleasant, when very quietly done. One must sit just under it. I still hate seeing the poor man who pulls it, whenever I go through the outer room, & so gladly give him a moment's rest.' But if Lady Canning had reservations about the working conditions of those employed to serve her, they were not shared by her two maids, Rain and West, who appeared to be enjoying the unaccustomed grandeur that their new circumstances gave them:

> Their carriage comes to the door every evening at six to take them out driving, but they are rather shy about it & do not much like going round in the ring on the course, & cannot stand being asked, 'Is that your carriage?' as it drives up every evening. Rain greatly delights in the command of the two tailors who work for me; a third even comes in to help, & they get through beautiful neat work in a wonderfully short time. They do not embroider: a 'chicken-wallah' comes for that, who works as well as the Irish. Another man, called a 'pen-wallah', comes every day to carry all muslins away to be ironed: so you can imagine that the maids live like ladies.

All the same, the two English maids did not find everything to their liking, and West, the younger of the two, proved difficult over the matter of sharing her room with lesser forms of animal and insect life. 'I had to move her and put her in one of the best spare rooms because two musk-rats and a centipede made life a burden to her downstairs.'

Once she had settled herself within her own secluded domain, Char began to explore further afield, looking at Calcutta and its inhabitants with a critical eye that reflected her own disappointment at its shortcomings. However, in what was

to be her fourth letter to the Queen she took care not to be too frank in her opinions:

> There is little to see here & the name of City of Palaces is presumptuous in a town of brick & plaster with poor native houses of Bamboo & mat, but it is an enormous place & the multitude of human beings is surprising. We ride about in all parts & very curious places we see. Only men & children are visible, very few even of very low caste women show themselves. The men are very often handsome & Spanish looking, Mahometans with their beards especially. Very wild figures of hill tribes are often seen. The soldiers are especially fine looking & seen to much the greatest advantage when out of their tight, unbecoming red coats & enveloped in their own white muslins. The body guard men are all above 6 ft. high and very handsome, and all have medals of battles.

The letter makes no mention of English society in Calcutta, but then so far as Charlotte Canning was concerned there really *was* no society as she understood it. Despite meeting large numbers of Calcutta dignitaries and their wives, she found herself 'isolated to a degree I never could have imagined'. As British India's First Lady she stood one rung above the wife of the Lieutenant-Governor of Bengal on the hierarchical ladder, two rungs above the wife of the Chief Justice and three above the wife of the Commander in Chief, Major-General George Anson. The consequence was that 'nobody speaks to me voluntarily'. On 19 March she was lamenting the fact that 'all the people here seem so afraid of me! and look alarmed when I go & sit by them & not one man has ever voluntarily spoken to me since I came to India, except General Anson and Sir J. Colvile. All the others I have actually to send for, or if they look tractable to beckon to come & speak to me & the ladies look terribly afraid. I begin to think I shall have to go my rounds like the Queen after dinner, only standing for one second is evidently thought quite indecorous here.' Large dinner parties given several times a week enabled the Cannings to get to know people but they were more often occasions to be endured rather than enjoyed:

> The plan here is for every one to come very early, long before they are asked, and no one to go till the greatest lady gets up to take leave; then all the others come up & bow in a flock, & off they go, & all are cleared away in two minutes, the ADCs handing the ladies. The ADCs also receive the ladies, and hand them in, but some shy ones still touchingly cling to their husbands and natural protectors, & look very absurd dragged up by two men.

The Cannings' only real friends in India during these first months were the Ansons, whom they had known well from earlier days in London society. The Governor of Bengal and his wife proved to be 'too Indian' for the Cannings' comfort, while

The 'most civilised room in India'; Lady Canning's private sitting-room at Government House, Calcutta, after six weeks of redecoration. Suspended from the ceiling are the fans known as punkahs.

the Chief Justice was a bachelor, so it was to General and Mrs Anson – themselves comparative newcomers to the Indian scene – that they mostly turned for companionship. A former Guards officer who had fought at Waterloo and afterwards had been a Member of Parliament for many years, George Anson was an aristocrat 'so imperturbably good tempered and so thoroughly a gentleman' that Charles Canning was later to find it difficult to quarrel with his bad judgement as a military commander. It was Mrs Anson who most frequently accompanied Char when she went out for the customary evening rides and it was at their house that the Cannings dined on one of their first evenings away from Government House: 'They had asked all the nicest people to meet us, and the drive there in the bright moonlight was quite a treat.' Yet the company failed to come up to Char's expectations:

> It is quite odd how, in an instant, one traces out the women who are not Indian, and who come of some good English county family; the difference is quite extraordinary. The Indian families – I do not mean half-caste or of Indian blood, but those who are always connected with India, & have only been sent home to be educated & had out again quite young – are more insipid than words can express, but they say so little, & I have so little to do with them, that I ought not to complain. I own, however, that the whole society is much duller than I could have conceived possible, & I look forward to the filling up of our staff with great interest.

Despite the limitations of Calcutta's social life and her own isolated position, Char soon came to know its conventions all too well. 'We call this a large society, but it really is not so', she explained in a letter to her mother, Lady Stuart de Rothesay:

> Every one knows who everybody is, except just the new-comers and people passing through. It is unlike even Dublin in that. Every really white person, except a very few shopkeepers, and sailors and soldiers, is by way of a gentleman or a lady, so there is little difficulty in knowing every really white face in the whole town. That is one of the curious things – never to see middle-class or poor people, except very dark half-castes and natives. A white woman on foot is almost an unknown sight, in a street quite unknown; on a cool evening a few, but very rarely, walk a little way on the course. So no wonder we all know each other's faces, and everybody knows what everybody does. Gossiping and evil-speaking is very common, I am told; so if there is bad to tell, it comes out soon enough. No one is intimate enough to gossip to me, so I cannot speak from experience. It is quite a mistake to suppose that the society here is bad. Even flirting is very rare and of the mildest description, and I really believe hardly any woman but me goes out riding without her husband. It is really a very proper place; its greatest sin is its intense dullness.

Char soon realised that for company she was going to have to rely a great deal on the aides-de-camp attached to her husband's staff, rather in the same way as the Queen relied for companionship on her ladies-in-waiting. The thought appalled her: 'Just imagine fishing out Captain Anybody from a regiment & going driving along the Serpentine with him. You have no idea how essential it is to get gentlemanlike good sort of Aides de Camp, for I foresee they will be my constant companions for the next five years.' However, help was on the way in the person of Charles Canning's nephew, thirty-year-old Ulick Canning de Burgh, Lord Dunkellin, 'prosperous & merry & bearded & red', who arrived in June fresh from the Crimea to take up the joint post of Military Secretary and ADC. He was to be followed in due course by other personable gentlemen-bachelors, all of whom helped to make life more agreeable for both the Governor-General and his lady.

Lord Dalhousie had described the power vested in a Governor-General as 'full-blown despotism', but if this authority was to be exercised responsibly it demanded an enormous sacrifice of time and energy. Canning willingly took up the challenge, acknowledging that a 'new Governor-General should be little better than a galley slave'. He at once threw himself into his work, starting at six every morning and, within a matter of days, had abandoned the customary Indian practice of going out for a short gallop before breakfast. Indeed, Char found it increasingly difficult to get him to take any exercise at all. 'His work is really too much for any one man', she lamented in her journal. 'C. is still against early exercise, but he always gets up and goes to his work at six. I think his military work comes heaviest upon

The Hindu temple of Kali at Kalighat, from which Calcutta derived its name, located on the southern outskirts of the city.

him – such endless enquiries, and cases of misconduct of the most troublesome kind.' The new telegraph lines, now stretching across India from Bombay to Calcutta and from Lucknow to Calcutta, added to the Governor-General's burden: 'The electric telegraph brings questions at all hours from Oude, requiring immediate answers, which must be a very interrupting way of doing business. Oude entails a good deal [of work], but it goes on quite smoothly. The former army accepts its arrears in pay, and the whole population accepts the change quietly, and readily benefits by it in a contented spirit.'

After breakfasting together the Cannings usually met again in the late afternoon when, if his work allowed it, Charles would join his wife for a 'slow dowagery' drive in their barouche out to the racecourse on the Maidan, 'where the whole English population rushes out for half-an-hour at sunset'. Being drawn 'round & round the course bowing to all the beau monde' was not an experience that either enjoyed. Infinitely more pleasurable were the rare occasions when they were able to ride out together and explore the less urbanised corners of the city. 'We had a charming ride in the lanes which had always looked tempting behind Alipore', begins Char's account of one such adventure:

> I believe they are in sort of fruit-grounds, & here & there a few thatched & matted huts are hidden amongst them. The whole is interspersed with ditches, & the square cool ponds always called 'tanks' here. Very often one sees a half-ruined tomb or temple. The trees meet overhead, & the lanes are often quite narrow, the undergrowth most luxuriant, arum leaves everywhere & often a sort of aloe or pine-apple. In one place we came upon a sort of camp of people bringing in hay, with little carts drawn by the usual bullocks with humps. It got dark long before we found our way back to the carriage by the intricate roads, & then the whole country was illuminated with fireflies, glancing about among the leaves & the grass, & to the top of the high bamboos & Indian figs. This little bit of variety was quite refreshing, like going away to another place.

But aside from such rare treats Char was finding her life exceedingly circumscribed. 'At present my solitude and idleness are unbounded, and it is anything but cheerful', she noted soon after her arrival. Three weeks later the situation was proving to be as wearisome as she had feared:

> It is provoking to feel so utterly useless, when C. is working like a horse. Mrs. Anson complains that she has not even house-bills to look at! That is 'le cadet de mes regrets', but I should like to be good for something. My personal life is absolutely uneventful. Putting dimity in a drawing-room or a new mat, is about the principal event I can look forward to: or choosing 30 names out of a list for dinner, and ditto two days later, and so on three times a week.

The cause of Char's difficulties was never directly expressed. During the eight years of Lord Dalhousie's extremely authoritarian regime Government House had lacked a commanding female figure – and now that Lord Canning was in charge he had no wish to rock the boat. 'C. is all for following precedent, and my independence is quite at an end', was all that Charlotte Canning was prepared to say on the subject.

As the Hot Weather began to bite, Charlotte's feeling of helplessness increased. 'We are beginning to feel real heat', she wrote on 3 April:

> The punkah on one's – usually damp – skin tells with great effect. I have not had it yet at night. It is 86° in my room now, 90½° when the windows are open at sunset: our dear old doctor goes about arranging our shutters and thermometers, and doing all he can to make us comfortable. It is rather a weary time, for I am so idle! and must be so. I never knew what idleness was before, but I cannot busy myself, even with books, as I used anywhere else. Even drawing

The northern boundary of the Calcutta Maidan, showing Government House as it was in 1859, engraved from a drawing by Major T. J. Ryves. The Cannings' private apartments were in the left wing of the south front, overlooking the Maidan.

> is a great deal of trouble, and the room is dark, and one does not feel much inclined. I was promised to see no more mosquitos when the heat began but I think they are worse than ever. We have dinners of meat killed in the morning, and everything that is light and crisp is very bad. I believe the cook's torments are great, and it is a wonder how he manages dinner at all.

Besides inducing lassitude, the heat also brought about a general loss of appetite. Within weeks Char's plump cheeks and double chin had vanished: 'I shall soon be a skeleton, and very yellow, like everybody here. The poor children are like tallow candles. C. grows thin too. All the same, I never was so well before.' Before the Cold Weather season began again in October the maids would be taking in her dresses a full four inches round the waist. When Lord Dunkellin arrived the Hot Weather was at its worst. In a cheerful letter to his father he described how he found the Cannings: 'I thought Aunt C. in great blow, looking very pretty and wonderfully well, tho' she has since persisted so strongly in saying how thin she has grown that I have become convinced of the fact, and she is also a little browned. Uncle C. was not looking so well. He is thinned and looks rather pasty.'

The gregarious Lord Dunkellin found the restrictions on social activity imposed by the Hot Weather extremely irksome. Certainly, the routine required to keep the interior of a house from heating up during the hours of sunlight was considerable. As soon as the sun was up the local equivalent of Venetian blinds, known as *jhilmils*, were closed. Large wetted grass screens called *tatis* were erected to enclose every verandah and balcony, so that no chink of light filtered through to the interior of the house. An hour or so later every window was closed, ensuring that the air within the darkened rooms – kept circulating by punkahs – remained at a more or less constant temperature throughout the day. Then as soon as the sun went down all doors, windows and blinds were thrown open, allowing the evening breezes to blow in what was initially the much warmer outside air, but which soon fell in temperature as dusk came on. 'No one', wrote Lord Dunkellin, 'dreams of going out unless on some particular business before 5.0 or 5.30 at the earliest.'

By the end of April Char's reservations about using the punkahs at night had vanished in the face of cruel experience: 'I slept very badly, and at last thought the world in general must have reason, and I need not deny myself what I find is a universal indulgence. The result has been that I sleep to perfection. It acted like magic. So now I am completely vanquished on the punkah point.' She was not alone in making compromises: 'I catch the body-guard sentries in the passages fanning themselves with hatchet-shaped palm-fans. It looks very absurd to see a great tall man, dressed in red like an English cavalry soldier, and probably covered in medals, fanning himself thus.'

As the Indian summer wore on other manifestations of the Hot Weather appeared:

> The heat has not increased but there are other signs of the climate. Insects are much commoner. Great cockroaches, as big as mice, are very common. They run along the floor, & now & then spread their wings & fly upon me! I let them alone, for I could on no account kill anything so big; but Rain has no mercy, & the other night killed five as I was undressing to go to bed. Some were moving away, side by side, like pairs of coach-horses. Small red ants are in such quantities that we are obliged to put the legs of the dressing-tables into little saucers of water. Enormous spiders, earwigs with wings, & various curious specimens of nondescript kinds, make up the collection.

Another indication of the Hot Weather was the increased risk of disease, cholera being the main hazard. 'There is cholera about', wrote Char in April. 'There are no drains anywhere, so no wonder it is never quite away. C. is out of patience when they talk of putting in gas before this absolute necessity is managed.' A month

Lady Canning's sitting-room at Government House, Barrackpore, with its thirteen doors and three windows, transformed by Charlotte's favourite blue stripe chintz with rosebuds on a white background. 'I am getting so fond of this place', she wrote in her journal on 22 October 1856. 'I believe it would look rather nice even as an English country-house, so marvellously is it improved by 450 yards of rose-chintz, a great many arm-chairs, small round tables, framed drawings etc, & flowerpots in number.'

ABOVE The Garden Reach at Barrackpore – 'where I can go & sit & breathe fresh air in the evening'.

OPPOSITE ABOVE Near the main gate at Barrackpore Park. 'This evening I had a most successful ride round a labyrinth of jungly lanes,' wrote Charlotte in her journal on 29 October. 'Here & there are brick walls & summer houses, those modern brick ruins which make such beautiful colouring in contrast with the intense green.'

BELOW 'I have had a good deal of amusement in cutting down shrubs & opening out vistas. Such a beautiful banyan tree, like a grove, covered with creepers & orchideous plants, is now exposed to view.' This banyan grove became one of the Charlotte Canning's favourite haunts at Barrackpore.

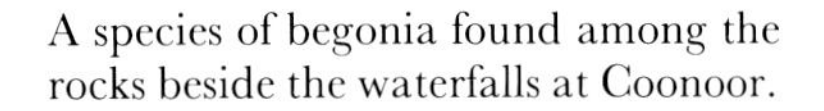
A species of begonia found among the rocks beside the waterfalls at Coonoor.

The 'fiddle-leafed' *Jatropha Pandurae-folia*, sketched at Barrackpore.

The popular *Aerides Multiflorum* orchid, brought down to Calcutta from Assam.

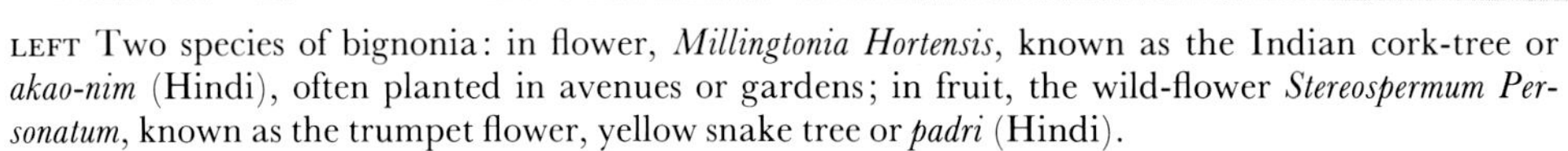
LEFT Two species of bignonia: in flower, *Millingtonia Hortensis*, known as the Indian cork-tree or *akao-nim* (Hindi), often planted in avenues or gardens; in fruit, the wild-flower *Stereospermum Personatum*, known as the trumpet flower, yellow snake tree or *padri* (Hindi).

RIGHT The fruit of the *kadamb* tree, *neolamarckia cadamba*, found in gardens throughout India.

later she was recording the death from cholera of the pretty young wife of a lieutenant of the bodyguard – 'they had twice dined with us'. One week later, on 20 May, there was another victim to report, this time much closer at home. It was the French chef, 'our poor cook, Monsieur Crepin', whom they had inherited from Lord Canning's predecessor. In the same entry Lady Canning admitted to a significant change of attitude: 'I am shocked at being hardened now to the feeling of giving work & trouble, that at first I minded so much. Now it never occurs to me to think of the punkah-man pulling at his rope. I believe they go to sleep, & when awake, do not mind; but it is a change for the worse in one's feeling.' For better or worse, she was becoming acclimatised, both physically and morally.

In that year of 1856 the Rains that ended the dry months of summer broke unusually early. On 14 May Char was prevented by the presence of visitors from taking her customary ride in the late-afternoon. After their departure she went out on to her balcony to read and, when the shutters had been opened, she watched from her commanding view the scene on the Maidan:

> The sky to the south was grey & not stormy; but suddenly a wind seemed to rise in the east, the world began to scamper away, & a dust-storm came on. All round the country the clouds of dust rose, & was carried along like thick smoke in violent east wind. Just before seven, I went to get C. to come & refresh himself with a walk in his colonnade. As soon as we got there I found inky clouds passing as fast as birds from the north, & in a few seconds they came down from the north-west in a hurricane, which lasted twenty-five minutes. The house shook, windows crashed & smashed, *gilmils* were blown in here & there. In my bedroom the windows had been left open, &, though the shutters were shut, the rain came in horizontally & drenched everything, even on the far side of the room, & left it ankle-deep in water, which rushed down the stairs in a cataract. Two inches of rain fell in the time – not half-an-hour. The blue lightning never ceased, but it was not forked, & I suppose not near, for I never heard the thunder – not that we could well have distinguished it from the roaring wind.

The storm created widespread havoc and produced 'adventures of the most wonderful kind to tell, some really frightful'. The Ansons were among the many Europeans caught out in the open:

> Whole families on horseback were run away with in different directions. Carriages without end were overturned, & the Grand Stand blown down. Mrs Anson's account of it all is wonderful – the screams of her daughter, & the screams of her dog, & the terrified horses running away, & all the other carriages turning over, & the trees crashing. Young Anson held by some rails, but, letting go for

an instant, was blown away an immense distance. A thousand dead crows were picked up by the Fort. On the river the damage has been frightful, and no one will ever know to what extent amongst the poor native boats.

All next day the lightning was more beautiful than anything I ever saw. First it was all white, as if strings of silver were thrown through the air quite horizontally; then in other places like lightning from the hand of Jupiter; in others like trees – sometimes like blue, sometimes pink. Looking out the river way, there was a lurid brown, red & olive sunset, & beautiful reflections, then ink-like clouds all round.

In early August Charlotte was writing to the Queen once more, providing a precis of the main events of the summer and detailing some of the effects of the monsoon: 'The greenness of Bengal surprised me even at first. Now it is quite dazzling & the beauty of the rank & gigantic foliage is indescribable. Your Majesty once pitied me for the heat & the insects I should encounter. At the beginning of the rains sometimes the dinner table was covered with thousands of insects of all kinds as thick as in the drawers of a collection. Silver covers had to be put on all the glasses & it was really a curious sight.' Char had asked for a collection of such insects to be assembled and sent off to the royal children for their museum at Osborne House. This first attempt failed when the specimens rotted in the intense humidity but Charlotte assured the Queen that she would persevere.

Her letter was not simply confined to descriptions of events and Indian exotica. Lady Canning had begun to make a study of Indian women and the problems of plural marriage and widowhood. The issue of women's education was again raised – and, at last, she had found something worthwhile to occupy at least part of her time: 'Ever since I arrived I have tried to find out if any particular duty might be within my province & I have only found that of visiting female schools. It is an agreeable one.' It was not much to build on, but it was a start.

CHAPTER III

'A Different Stage of Existence'

Buckingham Palace,
June 22nd, 1856

My dearest Lady Canning,
Over & over again I had intended to thank you for your two kind & most interesting letters . . . . I am now anxious to tell you that I wish you would write to me every six weeks – whether you hear from me or not, as it seems else so long not to hear from you. I must likewise remind Lord Canning that I have not heard from him yet – his Predecessor used to write to me sometimes every two or three months . . .

QUEEN Victoria's letter arrived in Calcutta exactly one month after posting – 'the shortest time ever known' – full as ever of homely chat about the royal offspring and the gracious life that Charlotte had left behind. The main family news was that the Princess Royal was now engaged to Prince Frederick William of Prussia (the future Kaiser Frederick), 'though – as the marriage is not to take place till after she is seventeen – it will not be officially or publicly announced until shortly before the time. The young people are extremely attached to each other & very happy together & he wonderfully in love!' The main item of general news was that the British troops were on their way back to Britain from the Crimea: 'The great event now looked forward to with much joy & impatience – is the return of my dear Guards – which is daily expected . . .'

Despite the Queen's reminder to Lord Canning that she should be kept regularly informed 'of the state of the Country – of our relations with the Native Princes, the finances & improvements', and despite Char's assurances that Lord Canning would 'not fail to avail himself of Your Majesty's gracious permission to him to write', the Queen had to wait seven months before she heard from her Governor-General in person. No snub was intended. What Lady Canning described as 'C.'s piles & pyramids & columns of boxes of work' were keeping him occupied from dawn till sunset, while the brief periods of relaxation that he allowed himself were steadily being reduced: 'C. hardly rides once or twice a week now, and the other

days he paces round and round the garden at a speed very good for him, but out of the question for me.'

As if to make up for her husband's silence, Char adhered strictly to the Queen's wishes. Her letters followed at regular six weekly intervals – until events in the following summer of 1857 imposed their own more urgent timetable. On 7 October she was able to inform Queen Victoria that a second attempt at putting together a collection of insects for the royal children, with 'drawers of butterflies, silkworm moths, centipedes, scorpions, tarantulas and all sorts of curious things', had succeeded and that they had been despatched via the Cape. The realisation that her letters were avidly read not only by the Queen but by those close to her was immensely gratifying. She became more relaxed in style and more confident in tone. In her October letter there was a graphic account of the way in which India's cycle of seasons dominated their lives:

> The Rains have almost ceased and we are longing for what is called the Cold Weather, the beginning of which is due in about ten days. Meanwhile the heat is more oppressive than ever. The inundations have been far beyond their natural heights & there is great distress in the upper part of Bengal. The cattle is seen crowded on every rising ground & standing in water half starved & many people are driven out of their huts or living on platforms within them. The Collectors [civil administrators] are everywhere desired to ascertain what can be done & much work will be given when the waters subside, but sickness & distress from loss of stores & cattle is inevitable & after all this they say there may be expected an enormous harvest next year. The actual loss of life is not supposed to be great as the rise of water is so gradual on that curious tract of flat land.

Beyond the Gangetic plains and so far unseen by the Cannings were the great mountain ranges of the Himalayas, whose foothills had all through the preceding months offered the promise of a refuge from the hot weather. Only two hill stations, where refugees from the plains might go to escape the heat, were well-established – at Simla and Mussoorie – but both were so far to the north-west as to be all but out of reach. However, Char had been hearing – and evidently thinking at some length – about another, newer hill station that was in the process of being developed, one which in the end was to prove a fatal lure:

> I have been hearing an account of the beauty & merits of a hill-station, Darjeeling, only about 350 miles from here but so inaccessible that it can hardly be reached in 10 days or a fortnight and a jungle, pestilential at some seasons, keeps people imprisoned in the hills rather than [take] the risk of a day or two in passing thro' it at foots pace in a Palanquin. In time the railway will be within 80 miles of it & a road in making to the summit itself.

Charlotte's interest in the Himalayas has been aroused by her meetings with the Superintendent of Calcutta's Botanic Garden, Dr Thomas Thomson, who had spent more than a decade exploring and collecting plants in the Western and Eastern Himalayas. They shared a common passion for plants and flowers. 'I squeeze out of him all the information I can', Lady Canning was later to write. 'He is most amiable in getting plants for me.' Dr Thomson had journeyed extensively in the mountains round Darjeeling in the company of the famous botanist Sir Joseph Hooker and was able to impart a great deal of first-hand information about its charms – and its dangers, for between the plains and the foothills there lay a wide belt of jungle known as the *terai* that was infested with malaria. What most appealed to Charlotte Canning, however, was the unique vantage point that Darjeeling provided:

> The highest mountain in the world was to be seen from it – but a higher still 60 miles further has been discovered of past 29000 ft. It was said to be without a name & the Geographers threatened to call it after the Surveyor Mt Everest, but nearer neighbours easily produced the local name & a very grand one: 'The Abode of the God' 'Deodunga' or 'Devadunga' – and another name which I forget also competes so we may hope the surveyor's [name] will be dropped.

This same letter also carried news of the Cannings' first move outside the boundaries of Calcutta for nearly seven months. The Governor-General had two official residences in Bengal. In Calcutta he occupied Government House but sixteen miles up-river he had his country residence at a place called Barrackpore (Barrackpur, today), taking its name from the military post established there in 1775. A house and grounds had been purchased across the river from the military cantonments for the Commander in Chief of the Bengal Army and in 1801 this had been appropriated by the then Governor-General, Lord Arthur Wellesley, for his country seat. Wellesley had set about laying the foundations for a companion piece to the palatial structure that he had just caused to be erected in Calcutta, but had been ordered to call a halt by the Directors of the East India Company. Wellesley and his successors had been forced to make do with a comparatively modest 'matter-of-course-looking place', a colonnaded villa set in what struck Charlotte Canning as 'the most English well-kept green park I ever saw'. Soon after their arrival in Bengal the Cannings had driven out to Barrackpore to inspect their country seat and had returned to Calcutta far from impressed. In July, however, their friends the Ansons went there for a fortnight and came back with some wonderful tales. 'Their jackal stories are really incredible', Char noted in her journal. 'How people and dogs were beset by them.'

The Cannings' second visit to Barrackpore in late September gave them a better

opportunity to look over the house and grounds. Since Lady Dalhousie's death four years earlier the main building had hardly been occupied, and as a result its interior furnishings had been greatly neglected. Moreover, it was too small to house any guests, which meant that they had to be accommodated in a number of simple thatch bungalows scattered through the grounds.

However, Barrackpore could offer something else that the Cannings had not hitherto found in India: peace and tranquillity. As Char soon discovered, its rural setting more than made up for the home's deficiencies. 'It is a large Park on the banks of the river very like Sion', she informed the Queen:

> The house is rather shabby for Lord Wellesley's grand projects were not sanctioned from home after he had finished Government House & intended to reproduce it here. I amuse myself with attempts to make this house comfortable &

The verandah at Government House, Barrackpore, looking out across the Hooghly. Painted in December 1856.

> enliven the drawing room by decorating it with framed sketches, & Your Majesty's last gifts of portraits are surrounded by recollections of Osborne & Balmoral & all my favourite spots at home. The plan of an Indian room is odd & not in English ideas of comfort. This [room] for instance has 13 doors with panels like Venetian blinds & 3 windows opening on a verandah, matted floors, white walls, ceilings of painted beams exposed to view, that the ravages of white ants may be instantly discovered.

But it was the grounds and their contents that were her great delight:

> The Park is carefully planted with round headed trees to look as English as possible — more so than I approve, and I am glad when Bamboos & Cocoanuts & Palms have crept in. All the apparent chestnut, elms & ash prove quite unknown on nearer view. The luxuriant growth in the jungly ground outside, of dazzling green during the Rains, is more beautiful than I can describe & I always think of the Palm House at Kew which gives a faint idea of it. I wish I knew the plants better but there is so little prospect of being out in real daylight & I cannot often indulge in very early rising as it is the thing that knocks me up.

As well as a formal pleasure garden complete with Grecian temples and Gothic ruins, Barrackpore Park also contained an animal menagerie inhabited by a giraffe, a tiger, a cheetah, a number of rhinoceros and some bears – one of which had been a pet of Lady Dalhousie's and liked to be fed on cakes. There was also a handsome aviary made up of 'Gothic arcades over tanks, chiefly stocked with water birds – a Chinese pigeon with a beautiful crest and blue slate-coloured plumage is my especial admiration'. The Governor-General's elephants for use on all state occasions were also housed in the Park. At one time they had numbered over a hundred but with the coming of the railways their usefulness as a means of conveyance on imperial progresses across the country had declined. On Charlotte Canning's first visit to the stud she found only eight of these 'most sensible gentle monsters'. One jolting ride was enough to convince her that travelling on elephant-back was 'amusing rather than agreeable'. Nevertheless, the elephants proved to be invaluable when it came to entertaining guests: 'I find a ride upon the elephants has a wonderfully reassuring effect upon people who arrive very much alarmed at us.'

Directly across the river from the Park were the headquarters of the Bengal Army, where a number of Indian infantry and cavalry units commanded by British officers were stationed. One evening soon after their arrival Char accompanied her husband on an inspection of these military cantonments: 'I never knew before what the meaning of cantonments was, or what they looked like. I believed it to be the exclusively military quarter. The officer's houses are exactly the same

'I find a ride upon the elephants has a wonderfully reassuring effect upon people who arrive very much alarmed at us.' Perhaps one of the few surviving photographs of the thousands taken by Lady Canning in India.

as other people's, with gardens, being bungalows of various shapes & sizes, some thatched & some cemented, with columns & verandahs. The gardens are all much gayer than ours. The soldiers' lines are small huts, and each regiment separate. A bazaar, of native huts, belongs to each. Only three regiments & a half are here now: formerly there were many more.' There was no British regiment stationed at Barrackpore. Indeed, in the whole of Bengal and Bihar there were only two battalions of British infantry, one in Calcutta, the other five hundred miles up-river at Dinapore (Dinapur, today). By contrast, there were more than fifty-five thousand Indian Company troops between Calcutta and Meerut. Such a discrepancy in numbers was considered perfectly normal; it was part of the phenomenon of British rule in India.

Only a month after their arrival at Barrackpore Char was noting in her journal how 'fond of the place' she was becoming. She had worked hard to imprint her style and taste on the house. The interior had been 'marvellously improved by 450 yards of rose-chintz, a great many arm-chairs, small round tables, framed drawings etc., & flower-pots in numbers. I really think I have now succeeded in equalling Parell [Government-House in Bombay] and could invite Elphy [Lord Elphinstone, Governor of Bombay] himself. It was quite amusing to do all this, and I came early in the morning to prepare for C., who had rather doubted finding any improvement & was enchanted.' Her next target was the exterior: 'I have now a great deal to improve out of doors, for the garden is badly laid out, though there is a charming terrace-walk by the river-side made by Lord Ellenborough. This, and a little ground along the edge, is all we have for private use, the rest is open to the public. I do not mind that, for it looks cheerful to see people, & the regiments send their bands to play in the evenings, & it has quite a gay effect.' What Lady Canning proposed to do was to remodel the terrace walk, taking as her model the terrace of her parents' home, Highcliffe Castle: 'The house faces a great reach of the river, & is crooked to the bank. I want to set it straight to the eye by making another walk at the same angle, & a bank down to the waterside, & I should get a seat on the water's edge of the most airy description. I have opened to view a beautiful bunyan, of late hidden by shrubs.'

In late October a letter arrived at Barrackpore from the Queen which told of her longing to experience at first hand something of the extraordinary life that Lady Canning was leading in India. The Queen asked about her visits to the Indian schools and wanted to know how her sketching was progressing: 'What endless subjects for the drawings you must be doing, no doubt you have been very busy with your pencil, what would I give to see some of your sketches?'

In spite of the hot weather Char had indeed managed quite a number of school inspections. One such visit, to a Central Native Girls' School run by European teachers, had taken place in early May. 'It is very small, but well managed', she had written:

> 25 Christian native girls are boarders, all dressed like ghosts in white shrouds, 25 or 30 small day-scholars the same – low-caste children, not Christians but reading the Bible. I went by myself along the lines of children with the teacher, making her translate to me her questions and the answers. These brown children, with their beautiful black, animal-like eyes, are very touching – so gentle, often so handsome. They were quite pleased to be taken notice of. Then we went into the infant school of the same concern – 50 children in a gallery, each in the smallest loose little shift, without sleeves. A few were wretched little scarecrows, but the majority had enormous fat, hard, beautifully-made limbs, like bronze putti.
>
> They go away young, but this infant teaching and good discipline saves much

time when they get promoted to more important things. Yet these poor little low-caste girls can only marry bheesties, ie naked water-carriers, or meters – sweepers, quite as low.

Two weeks later Char had gone to see a European Girls' Orphan School:

> The girls are orphans, not only of soldiers, but of all English people, and they are very respectably brought up, in the National School style. I asked some questions, apropos to which it came out that each girl was expected to have her 18 suits of clothes complete, from her white calico frock downwards, everything clean every day. How that would astonish poor children in England! Their food costs next to nothing and this cotton very little, so it is all cheaply done — but what habits to carry to England!

Both these visits were made in the cool of the morning before breakfast but to Char's great irritation she found it impossible to avoid the protocol that such excursions inevitably entailed. 'Alas!', she recorded. 'My going to such places makes such an affair that I cannot do it very often. The state appearance of the carriage-and-four and body-guard makes such a sensation that it puts a school quite into

Government House, Barrackpore, as seen from the cantonment side of the Hooghly River.

The main gate at Barrackpore Park, sketched during the Cannings' first visit in March 1856.

fashion in the neighbourhood. I have quite made up my mind that I can only go about like an inspector at long intervals.'

That Charlotte Canning could go out on such early morning forays in the hottest month of the year makes her failure to pursue her chief interests all the more puzzling – for the fact was that she had done virtually no sketching or painting since her arrival in Calcutta. Nor had she so much as unpacked the photographic equipment that she had brought out to India with her. Indulging in either of these hobbies was 'out of the question', she had declared in one of her letters home, offering the heat and the lack of light as the excuse. However, the arrival of the Queen's letter seems to have coincided with a change of attitude on Lady Canning's part.

In mid-October Charles Canning moved back to Calcutta. He was finding Barrackpore too isolated for his work and the daily commuting to and from the city by coach took up too much of his time. Lady Canning chose to remain behind in Barrackpore. The Cold Weather had at last brought a temperate climate to Bengal and for the first time since her arrival she found herself free to get out and about at will. In this more relaxed atmosphere her spirits rose and she threw off the terrible inertia that had clung to her all through the preceding months:

C. went to Calcutta on Thursday, leaving me under charge of Captain Bowles. I took the opportunity of a ride to explore lanes, & found some beautiful ones full of fern, & came out at the place where all the elephants live – an enormous line of these giants piqueted on either side of their stable, a great many more than I had seen before. One, with his howdah and scarlet trappings, was in the middle of the stable compound, with all the horses going round and round in a long string in procession, to get used to him. Next morning I made an attempt to sketch. It was dark when I got up, & dull & grey when I chose my site, & I felt ill-disposed; but when the sun showed itself, I was quite surprised at the wonderful beauty of detail – all the tangle, & great unbroken leaves, & creepers & stems, all lovely to draw.

It was almost as though a spell had been broken. Char found herself once more

The jungle at Barrackpore. 'With C. I rode round some lovely paths through jungly groves – of mango, bamboo, cocoa-nut, plantains, arums etc, paths branching off in all directions, little huts, now & then small temples, ruined gardens; great sameness perhaps, but such beauty.'

putting her drawing skills to use, concentrating on flowers and foliage to begin with, selecting some branch or stem that caught her eye during her early morning ride and then sketching and painting it at leisure on her verandah later in the day. 'We walked to look at a tree called pterocarpus', begins a characteristic entry in her journal, dated 26 October. 'The foliage is like that of a weeping ash, only of far more beautiful quality, long flat branches of leaves shutting out the light, & yet quite thin. It is like one of Ruskin's specimens of an ill-drawn tree, so thick & even, & the stem like that of a beautiful chestnut.'

Another obvious subject at Barrackpore for both pencil and pen was the river, always brimming with traffic and human activity: '29 October. A squally day, the river covered with picturesque boats sailing up, & letting their ragged sails fly as the squalls come up.' The popular autumn festival of Durga Puja was now being widely and noisily celebrated by Hindus throughout the land. Bells, drums and fireworks could be heard from across the river and occasionally processions could be seen accompanying images of gods on palanquins along the bank. This was an aspect of Indian life that Charlotte, in common with many Europeans in India at that time, found most disquieting:

> We met gods & goddesses in crowds, carried on people's shoulders – horrid sort of yellow dolls of all sizes, dressed in tinsel, & invariably riding astride of peacocks with enormous spread-out tails. Sometimes twenty of these were carried along at once with music & drums. They usually voluntarily stopped their drumming as we passed, but not always, & I thought the horses very patient to bear such sights & sounds. I observed the gods all faced one way, in whichever direction they were carried – such dreadful creatures – I cannot imagine how any human being can respect them.

Despite her repugnance, Char found herself becoming increasingly drawn towards the picturesque scenes of native life – and death – that were to be seen being played out beside the Ganges. She witnessed cremations at the local burning ghat and returned several times to sketch at the nearby temple. On one such occasion she noted, with a painter's vision, how the evening light had turned sky and water into 'the same pale golden colour, an effect quite impossible to give, the trees like green tinsel, or green flies, or enamel'. She noted, too, that 'the great pair of scales near the spot turns out to be for weighing wood to sell for burning bodies, & the little three-roomed building for dying people who have a chance of life, & are allowed to take advantage of it. If carried down to the water's edge, they are not allowed to recover. If they do, they are treated as outcasts, the idea being that the river rejects them, & that they are utterly cast away from salvation.'

Such curious bits of information usually came from one or other of the eight officers that the Governor-General had on his official staff, made up of a Private Secretary, a Military Secretary, a surgeon and his five aides-de-camp. The most constant figure among them was the surgeon, Dr Leckie, who had been with Lord Dalhousie and was to remain with Lord Canning for the first five years of his period of office. He was a quiet and unobtrusive person with a fund of stories about India and its ways:

> Dr Leckie has more than once prevented people from being carried to the water's edge. A Ranee [queen] of Benares who was in a fit of cholera taken to the palace near the water, was recovered by him, & has kept up the greatest friendship ever since. This Ranee he was allowed to see; but the Queen of Oude he used to prescribe for less easily, only a hand poked through a hole in a curtain was permitted, or, if he made a push to see more of his patient, she was allowed to show her tongue through the hole!

The Indian Cold Weather was now at its best, providing clear sunny days followed by nights that had just a touch of chill about them, sometimes even bringing a raw fog and necessitating *chuddas* or shawls on beds: 'I had no sheet even all the Hot Weather, then a light cotton upper sheet when it grew moderate, then no punkah, and this chudda is now the fourth stage. I do not foresee coming to an English blanket yet.' But despite the drop in temperature Charlotte Canning continued to regard the Indian climate with mistrust. 'We have passed into a different stage of existence here', she wrote to the Queen on 23 November:

> The Cold Weather, as it is called, has set in – it is the time for flowers to bloom & for fruits, & for everything else like winter in cooler climates, but the air is fresh in mornings & evenings – the thermometer under 70 and a cheering refreshing sensation comes over one. Now the Punkahs are taken down and it is possible to move more out in the air – but the sun is still to be feared, its power is mysterious & it is odd why idle people sauntering about have 'coup de soleil' when they venture much into it & excited cricket players, tiger shooters, hunters of wild boar & even busy indigo planters do not mind it at all. Everyone has a 'solar' hat made of the pith of a tree which is an excellent non-conductor of heat.

Christmas came and went and with the start of the new year of 1857 it was back to the city in order that the Cannings might preside over the Calcutta 'Season', with its balls, race meetings and other social gatherings. Char was sorry to leave Barrackpore but, as she explained to the Queen, she made the most of the return journey to Calcutta:

> It occurred to me that I should like to come by water, instead of the road & I was fully repaid for the river's banks are beautiful, quite flat but so well wooded with large trees intermingled with Cocoa trees & Palm, & there are many quaint

The burning ghat at Barrackpore, where Charlotte came to sketch one Monday morning in January 1857.

> temples with the broad flights of steps into the river which are peculiar to India & of such a grand character. However, boating is not quite a pleasure, for one's senses are cruelly offended by the numbers of floating bodies of Hindoos who travel up & down with the tide until they entirely disappear. This holy river is thought the happiest of resting places but a mean propensity to economy in the wood of funerals causes many bodies to be launched into the water when hardly scorched. What would English Sanitary Boards say to these practices!

She went on to describe some of the highlights of the Calcutta Season: 'At the New Year's Day ball we had invitations sent to 1050 people. All the Native Princes living in & near Calcutta came in their finery – the Ameers of Sinde, Shere Singh & his brother, Prince Gholam Mahamed & sons & grandfather, and several other Rajahs of small states.'

There was more about the native princes – a subject particularly dear to Queen Victoria's heart – in Lady Canning's next letter, written during the official visit to Calcutta of the most powerful of the Maratha princes, Maharaja Madhavrao Scindia of Gwalior. The Maratha warrior-princes of Central India – Scindia of Gwalior, Holkar of Indore, the Gaekwar of Baroda and others – had been the Company's chief rivals in the struggle for supremacy in India thirty years earlier. Although beaten into submission they were by no means a spent force and their

continuing friendship was seen as vital to the future security of British India. No effort was spared to ensure that the Maharaja was given every respect due to him and royally entertained. The proceedings began with a splendid durbar which Char, seeing through a hole in a screen, thought amusing and thoroughly Eastern:

> The etiquettes are arranged with exceeding precision & in this case Lord Canning had to meet the rajah at the extreme end of the carpet & lead him up to a chair on his right. A conversation is then carried on by interpreters & then came the presents, the 51 trays of things all being laid before the rajah on the floor till it was covered. He had jewels, shawls, brocades & clocks, pistols, guns and I believe elephants & horses besides. Then the pearl necklaces were put on these visitors and the turn arrived for the usual salaam of the Calcutta natives, each coming up with some gold pieces in handkerchiefs as offerings. They are merely touched & the original proprietor returns them to his pocket.

The durbar ended with the usual distribution of *paan* to chew and the sprinkling of attar of roses on handkerchiefs. A few days later there was a second durbar at which Lord Canning and the Members in Council who made up his cabinet returned the Maharaja's visit: 'They all came back in pearl necklaces of different degrees, C.'s very large & showy, but of rather misshapen pearls & emeralds, and the youngest ADC's very poor and small, in the same pattern. The officer of the body-guard, trotting along, broke his thread, and his pearls were scattered on the road. These fine things all go at once to the treasurer.' A magnificent ball, with the Maharaja present as guest of honour, dressed in the plainest white silk and seated on a sofa in his stockings, ended the visit. 'So ends the Carnival', wrote Char in her journal. Two days later she noted that it was 1 March, the anniversary of their arrival in Calcutta:

> It is difficult to believe it is a year, and yet I always feel as if it was a lifetime, & I had never been anywhere else. It is very monotonous & sometimes very dull, but not without a great deal to interest one, too, & a great deal to see with one's eyes, when one has an opportunity for looking. But day after day I ride the same way, & see the same people & the same carriages & ships & buggys, & say 'How Mrs This is looking,' & 'How Mrs That's horse goes,' & it is very dull.

But already the chain of events that within a matter of weeks would engulf much of Northern India in a year-long nightmare of civil war, of massacre piled on massacre, had been set in motion. March 1857 began the Hindu year which marked the centenary of Clive's decisive victory at Plassey – and it had been prophesied that the British Raj in India would endure only for a hundred years. At Barrackpore and at other cantonments up and down Bengal the sepoys had begun to voice their opposition to Company rule. The mutiny had begun.

CHAPTER IV

'Burning and Murdering and Horrors'

Calcutta May 19 1857

Madam,
This mail will take to your Majesty some very sad accounts of the strange and terrible outbreaks in the last 9 days at Meerut & Delhi. Lord Canning would have wished much to write to your Majesty himself: but the telegraph messages which reach him incessantly, often several in an hour, on which he has to act and write his orders at once, will I fear not leave him a moment before the departure of the mail today.

As yet few details have been received of all these sad events, for there has only been time to hear of the beginning of the insurrection at Meerut by letter, and all else is reported by telegraph.

On the evening of Sunday 10 May *sowars* of the 3rd Light Cavalry had brought terror and devastation to the sprawling cantonment town of Meerut. In what appeared to be a spontaneous uprising, they had swept through the civil and military lines, slaughtering as they went and firing bungalows, before galloping off virtually unopposed towards Delhi, thirty-five miles to the south-west. Arriving at dawn at the old capital of the Mughals, the mutineers had swarmed across the river Jumna (Yamuna, today) and up to the Red Fort, sepoys from other Indian regiments swelling their numbers as they advanced. Eighty-two-year-old Mohammed Bahadur Shah, last of the Mughal line and existing quite contentedly on a pension from the East India Company, had been dragged from his couch and informed that he was once more Emperor of India. Outside the walls of the city English and Eurasian families in the civil lines were hunted down and killed. A brief message of alarm, tapped out on the telegraph before the lines were cut and passed on from station to station, at last had brought the news to Calcutta that disaster threatened to overwhelm every Briton in India.

The portents had been there for all to observe for months – but they had either been disregarded or underrated. Six weeks before the Meerut outrage Char had sent the Queen a long account of the disbanding on Barrackpore parade ground of a Hindu regiment whose men had refused to handle new cartridges which they believed to be polluted with cow's grease. This event had itself been preceded by other incidents that Charlotte had recorded in her journal. The brigade commander at Barrackpore was Sir John Hearsey, a dashing old sepoy general whom the Cannings had got to know well during their residence at Barrackpore. The General prided himself on his rapport with his troops and on 11 February Char had noted that he made a 'good little speech' to calm the fears of the men of the 2nd Native Infantry 'who are supposed to be rather disaffected on account of the new Minie cartridges, of which they complain on the ground that the grease used in making them up is suet-beef, and that they cannot touch. There have been mysterious fires at all the places where detachments of this regiment have been quartered.' But the handling of greased cartridges was not the only cause of alarm among the Indian troops. Their real fear was of religious conversion: 'Another rumour arose that the five men ordered from each regiment to Dum-Dum to learn Minie rifle practice, were brought there to be baptised.' Then there was the strange business of the unleavened bread known as chapattis:

> There is an odd, mysterious thing going on, still unexplained. It is this. In one part of the country the native police have been making little cakes – 'chupattis' – and sending them on from place to place. Each man makes twelve, keeps two, and sends away ten to ten men, who make twelve more each, and they spread all over the country. No one can discover any meaning in it.

On 26 February men of the 19th Native Infantry refused their cartridges. 'Sepoys are the most tractable good people', explained Char in her letter to the Queen, 'but any fear that religion or caste shall be tampered with, can always excite them to every possible folly.' Here again it was not only the issue of polluted cartridges that had provoked them:

> The obnoxious cartridges were withdrawn, & sepoys told to find grease for themselves, but the notion that their caste was to be broken, & that they must become Christian, spread widely. At least that is the pretended grievance & many most ridiculous stories were invented to support of the rumour. One being that Lord Canning signed a bond to Your Majesty that he would make them all Christian in 3 years.

Absurd as these notions appeared to many, Queen Victoria made it plain in her reply to Lady Canning that she could sympathise with those whom she regarded as *her* sepoys. 'There is a dangerous spirit amongst the Native Troops', she admitted. However, 'a fear of their religion being tampered with is at the bottom of it. I think that the greatest care ought to be taken not to interfere with their religion – as once a cry of that kind is raised amongst a fanatical people – very strictly attached to their religion – there is no knowing what it may lead to & where it may end.'

That attempts to interfere with their religious practices were certainly being made is well-illustrated by an example recorded by Lady Canning in her journal on 3 April, when she was writing about two other Indian regiments at Barrackpore also 'known to be much disaffected'. One of these was the 34th Native Infantry, commanded by a colonel determined to advance his religion at every opportunity:

> Colonel Wheler of the 34th is terribly given to preach; so even when he does not actually preach to his men (which some say he does, telling them they must inevitably become Christian), he must keep alive the idea that they have not full liberty of conscience. Old General Hearsey, who has the language at his finger-ends, on the other hand, has again and again made his speech that our religion is in our Book, and that he would not have any one be a Christian who does not know what is in our Book.

Sept. 8. 1857
Dear Lady Canning

Letters from the Queen, some showing signs of the fire that destroyed Lady Canning's tent in December 1859.

Not surprisingly, it was from the ranks of the 34th NI that the first individual mutineer appeared, a sepoy named Mangal Pande:

> A 34th man at Barrackpore made himself drunk with bang [cannabis], took a sword and musket, & regularly 'ran amuck'. He wounded a sergeant, then stabbed the adjutant's horse & killed him, & wounded the adjutant, who was still entangled with his fallen horse. Some of the guard refused to seize him, but General Hearsey came out, & the man, who was raging about quite mad, was at last taken, having just at that moment shot himself. He has since recovered, and will live to be hanged.

Further details of this incident and the part played by General Hearsey, whose decisive action stemmed the violence at its source, were relayed to Lady Canning some days later:

> When they were told to seize the Mongul Pandy, the Colonel could not make

Sepoys of the Bengal Native Infantry photographed in Lucknow by Ahmed Ali Khan shortly before the outbreak of the Mutiny.

> them stir, & poor Colonel Wheler gave it up: General Hearsey they obeyed directly. The man knelt down & levelled his musket at the General. His affectionate sons were on both sides, & one exclaimed, 'Take care, papa. Papa, he's potting at you,' a modern piece of slang, meaning shooting a sitting bird, hardly by fair means. C. laughed so at [being told] this.

This account of the affair came directly from the General, who had come to confer with Charles Canning at Government House. Char set it down in her journal on 11 May, having gone out to Barrackpore by herself for a couple of days, 'a little grumbling at C. for not giving himself even that change of air & semblance of holiday'. That same evening news was brought to the house of the Meerut mutiny twenty-four hours earlier: 'I never saw this telegraph, but it told of burning houses & fighting, & that the telegraph wire was cut, & the men escaped towards Delhi, & that they had released their comrades.' Packing up their bags, she and her party returned to Calcutta next morning.

The assumption in Calcutta was that the outbreak at Meerut would quickly be brought under control. It took time for the extent of the disaster to become known:

> May 13. In the morning a merchant brought a quantity of native ornaments for us to choose from to be sent to the treasury for presents. C. came up to breakfast, & quickly made a choice & sent the man away, & soon put such frivolities out of my head by showing me a terrible telegraph from Mr. Colvin, Lieutenant-Governor [of the North-West Provinces] at Agra. It was vague, & one hoped exaggerated. The reports came chiefly from an engineer who had escaped from some place on the way to Delhi, & he spoke of the revolted troops having gone on there; that the Commissioner, Mr. Fraser, & Captain Douglas were murdered, & all the Europeans said to be massacred.
>
> Later came a far worse telegraph, saying the King of Delhi had sent over to Agra to say the regiments had sided with the insurgents & that the town was in their hands. The report that all Europeans were murdered was confirmed.
>
> I had a quiet drive with Major Bowie & learnt much more than I knew before about Delhi. There never is a European regiment at Delhi, & yet the arsenal & magazine are there.

It was during this drive with the most experienced of her husband's ADCs that Char realised for the first time how extraordinarily vulnerable was their position from a military point of view. Most of the British troops in India were up in the Punjab, the nearest many days' march from Delhi. In Bengal their numbers had been strengthened by the arrival of the 84th Foot, brought over from Rangoon at Lord Canning's request specifically to preside over the disbanding at Barrack-

pore, but to all intents they were at the mercy of the many Indian regiments in Bengal whose loyalties could no longer be guaranteed: 'There are very few European regiments in the valley of the Ganges. After Barrackpore, there is only one at Dinapore, none at Allahabad, Patna, Benares, Cawnpore. Meerut is the greatest strength of all, & yet that has been unable, in the suddenness of the outbreak, to prevent burning & murdering & horrors.'

The situation was still very confused when Lady Canning wrote her sad letter to the Queen nine days after the Meerut uprising: 'We do not yet know the extent of the loss of the English residents & officers in the towns & cantonments. Every day news arrives of a few who have escaped. The details will surely be full of horrors and the suspense and anxiety of friends is very great.' However, Char was determined to put a brave face on things. 'There is no reason for alarm in this part of the country', she informed the Queen:

> Good reports continue to come in of the great towns, where there are no European troops, & for which most anxiety has been felt, such as those strongholds of Hindoo fanatics and Mussalmans [Muslims], Benares and Allahabad. The Lieutenant-Governor of the North West Provinces at Agra reports constantly that all is quiet there and seems full of confidence & good hope and very spirited & cheering messages arrive even from Lucknow, from Sir Henry Lawrence, who is indeed admirably suited for his difficult position.

With its 'idle chiefs & late oppressors of the people' eager to see themselves restored to power, Oude was not expected to remain loyal – especially since many of the sepoys of the disbanded regiments had their homes there. But other doubtful regions showed no signs of wavering: 'It has been a matter of real gratification to Lord Canning to receive the very cordial & loyal support of our late guest, Scindia [Maharaja of Gwalior], who entreated to be allowed to send his Body Guard, which is quite his pride & delight, & his favourite horse battery, to Agra. This, as a token of goodwill, was readily accepted, and his example has been followed by the Rajah of Bhurtpore (Bharatpur) and other smaller neighbouring Rajahs who have shown excellent feeling.'

Even as Lady Canning signed and sealed this letter more bad news was pouring in to the Governor-General's office downstairs: 'I find a heap of telegraphs from interior stations: very bad indeed in general. All Oude seems risen. Only Lucknow and Cawnpore and Allahabad are held. I cannot tell how many poor people implore the help of 100 or 200 Europeans. But, till the Delhi force is released, there is no possibility of giving more help. Every man is pushed up who can be sent – by bullock trains, steamers and dak [staging post] carriages.'

The position in which the Governor-General now found himself was not an

enviable one. Within the space of nine days he had lost control of a large portion of his dominions and a broad wedge of enemy territory had been driven between the Punjab and Bengal, splitting his already inadequate British forces. His indecisiveness over the release of a proclamation announcing that the Company Raj had no designs on native religion was widely regarded as a fatal delay. It was being put about that not only was Canning personally responsible for the present situation but that his continuing prevarication was preventing a speedy resolution of the crisis. The 'greatest grievance against C.', as Char saw it, was that 'he trusted the Sepoy regiments until he had reason to know they were not trustworthy'. But what alternative had there been – for 'with such a very small European force as we had, how could we hurry on the mutiny and exasperate the whole army by declaring war against it? And how could we bid them lay down their arms without strength to enforce it?' Every English newspaper in the land now carried 'savage articles' attacking the Governor-General and his administration and, as Char surmised all too accurately, 'they threaten, of course, that much worse are sent home'. The hunt was on for a scapegoat.

Much of this criticism was misplaced. The underlying causes of the mutiny had as much to do with the expansionist policies of Canning's predecessor and with current British notions of religious and racial superiority as with such incidents as the mishandling of the cartridges issue. Canning had inherited a situation that he knew to be precarious – but his pleas to be allowed to increase the number of British troops in India and reduce the Indian troops accordingly had been rejected by the home government on the grounds of cost. It was true, however, that he gave the appearance of indecisiveness. 'The Scotch element in his character perhaps inclined him to pause too long and too cautiously before determining his course in weighty questions', was the judgement of L. B. Bowring, his Military Secretary at a later date. 'This often gave rise to the appearance of irresolution in his decisions.' But when faced by a crisis, as Canning was in the second week of May 1857, he could and did act decisively. As soon as the extent of the calamity became clear he telegraphed Madras, Bombay and Pegu for troops and, acting entirely on his own responsibility, he despatched steamers to Ceylon and Singapore to intercept and divert a large punitive expedition under the political command of Lord Elgin that was then on its way to China.

There was also the entirely novel phenomenon of waging war across a subcontinent with the aid of the electric telegraph. This was the first campaign ever fought with modern systems of more-or-less instant communications over long distances and it had its drawbacks as well as its advantages. Conflicting reports from scores of up-country stations flooded in to the telegraph office at all hours of the day and night and the difficulty of maintaining links over enormous distances made it extraordinarily hard to keep track of what was going on. At the start of the Hot Weather General Anson, together with his entire headquarters staff and a number of British troops, had disappeared to Simla and to other hill stations in the Himalayan foothills. He put no faith in the telegraph and so for some days after the start of the crisis it proved impossible to locate him. When contact was finally established the Commander in Chief proved to be maddeningly slow in grouping his forces. After the fiasco at Meerut, Anson was determined to advance on Delhi with a force substantial enough to break the mutineers. He lacked not only troops but also arms and ammunition and the means to move them across country. A more imaginative or younger commander might have taken the risk and advanced at speed, but Anson thought otherwise and to the mounting concern of Canning and his advisers in Calcutta he took a month to prepare his Delhi Field Force for action.

Such problems were not understood or appreciated by the largely civilian population of Calcutta. Rumours were rife and both Indians and Europeans alike began to fear for their own safety. 'The panic here becomes very foolish', wrote Char scornfully in her journal:

> Revolvers are bought by everyone, & the Freemasons & clerks, & employees of all kinds, want to be formed into regiments & yeomanry. There is not the least cause of fear here, & it is absurd to see how people who ought to know better set an example of fear, which must have a bad effect on natives. Many people wish us to put off the ball on the Queen's Birthday – the 25th. I would not for an instant suggest such a thing. It may not be a cheerful ball in this time of anxiety, but we ought not to appear in a state of mourning for this temporary outbreak, & above all things not to seem to give in to the Indian notion of Delhi being the capital.
>
> Very Pickwickian remarks are sent in, such as a report from an officer that he 'saw no soldiers bathing this morning'. There are stories of prophecies of Brahmins of our rule lasting a hundred years and other stories about the fall of Brahminism, & that Jupiter and Venus were this year foreboding its last chance. Some people come and ask if we go to sleep every night in the Fort, or if we have a hundred Europeans to guard us. We do everything as usual, and have the body guard and the 2nd [Bombay] Grenadiers. The body guard, fine tall picked men, with three or four medals apiece, are, I am sure, entirely trustworthy, & they laugh at the cartridge stories.

As the Queen's Birthday approached more doubts were raised over the wisdom of allowing Indian troops to take part in the firing of the tradition *feu-de-joie*, in

OPPOSITE Charles Canning reading military despatches.

CHINA COAST

which each soldier fired in turn to produce a rapid blaze of firing down the line: 'Many wise heads warn C. against it, because blank cartridges must be served out to 250 of the native regiment in the Fort.' The Cannings thought these objections absurd. 'Any mistrust shown or differences made, C. thinks would be most unwise.' In the event, their confidence in the Indian troops was not shaken:

> May 25. The Queen's Birthday. The morning guns from the Fort and steamer woke me, & I listened to the salute at real daylight, & hurried to a south window to try & see what happened at the feu-de-joie. The Queen's 53rd was drawn up like a red wall on the rampart facing this way, & the native regiment, in its white summer clothing, continued the line. The dotted lines of flashes went duly from end to end, long before I could hear the sound, but I knew then all had gone rightly.
>
> And so passed this much dreaded birthday. The ball was a very fair one, considering all the absurd stories circulated to frighten away the guests. I believe about 650 people came.

The Queen's Birthday more or less coincided with the disembarkation in Calcutta of the first reinforcements, the Madras Fusiliers, led by the redoubtable Colonel James George Neill, a puritanical Scot of ferocious temperament who brooked no nonsense from anybody. His men, 'Neill's Blue Caps', were equally hard-bitten, most of them volunteers of British stock drawn from Madras's 'poor white' community. This same regiment had played the leading role in the battle of Plassey, when a thousand British soldiers with two thousand Indian sepoys had routed an army twenty times their size, so its arrival had certain symbolic overtones that did a lot to counter the now common belief among Indians that the days of British rule were numbered. 'Some doubt for the moment about paying their rent', noted Charlotte: That is no great wonder, for they are inclined to say the 'Raj of the Company is ended' – Raj is royalty or supreme power. A great many say it is to end on the 23rd, the anniversary of Plassey, one hundred years ago. We say we shall be all right again by that day, and we have got the identical regiment that won it for Lord Clive! – the 1st Madras Fusileers!

The Madras Fusiliers were at once despatched up-country on the hundred miles of working railway that was in operation between Calcutta and Raniganj, although not before thoroughly frightening the stationmaster and his staff. 'They had a decided character in their Colonel,' wrote Charlotte, 'for when part had arrived at the railway station, & the station-master wanted to start the train without the rest, he fixed bayonets & held the whole station establishment under arrest till all the men were seated in the carriages, & would not listen to the protestations of the engineers, who declared their engine would burst.'

Next day the telegraph brought more bad news: 'All yesterday we were in great suspense from telegraphs hinting at "a most sad event". For a moment we doubted it but today the full account is come, & it is true that General Anson has died of the cholera!' It was with this sad news that Charlotte began her next letter to Queen Victoria, written on 5 June. The rest of what she had to impart was hardly more cheerful:

> The state of things in the north west is little changed since last mail – the suspense has been long and trying, and many regiments have fallen away; but it is surprising how many doubtful places have remained quiet & kept in check by very small European forces and the prudent arrangement & boldness of the authorities. All the great towns in the valley of the Ganges about which so much anxiety was felt, have remained quiet & a violent outbreak at Lucknow and the defection of several regiments did not inflame the country.
>
> The stories of the sudden & capricious changes of several regiments are most strange. The 9th was believed to be excellent, it had guarded Ld. Dalhousie's camp all over the country. A Brahmin came & preached mutiny and massacre of Europeans, the men seized him & gave him up, he was tried & some of the natives condemned & hung him. Just after a Brahmin stepped out of the ranks & said he was a martyr & he should like to be hung too! Then they all declared they could no longer obey their officers and they took possession of Allyghur & soon joined the rest at Delhi.

Great store was being set on the recapture of Delhi and the failure of the Delhi Field Force to advance was hard to explain. 'It is doubtless with a view of neglecting no precaution to ensure success that so large a force has been collected and so much delay caused', Lady Canning suggested, going on to explain why it was that the various relief columns were so slow in moving up-country:

> The Hoogly is low at this season and the flat boats towed by steamers have to reach the Great Ganges by another branch making a long circuit. It takes 25 days even to reach Benares! Lord Canning has made use of every device for conveying men speedily, even by forwarding very small detachments 18 & 24 daily by all the fast dak travelling carriages, little vehicles drawn by one horse & bullock trains carry 100 a day at the rate of 30 miles. All this makes one long for the completion of the railways. The telegraph has been of the greatest use but now is stopped in many important places.

The first flurry of telegraphed accounts of uprising and disaster was now giving

way to longer and more accurate despatches. Char was able to provide the Queen with several instances of great bravery and kindness performed by Indians:

> I am told of some marvellous escapes. Some officers actually had to swim the Jumna helping the poor ladies across as they fled from the massacre at Delhi. Then they wandered in the jungles & were robbed of all, till at last a Christian zemindar [landowner] found and befriended them & sent for some cavalry to rescue and escort them. Many servants behaved nobly. Mrs Greathed at Meerut was saved by her Ayah who begged her not to run away but to go to the top of the house. She then went down, opened all the doors & windows & waited for the rebels, then told them that the master and mistress had not waited for them but went off long ago, so they set the house on fire and left it. She then got the poor lady down from the burning house & hid her all night in the garden. Another ayah saved the three poor babes of a Mrs Hamilton, whose death was so terrible, by tying them up in a shawl which she carried on her back & she kept them in the bazaar till a friend recognised them.

When three weeks later Charlotte Canning sat down to write her next letter to the Queen, Calcutta was still in a state of jitters as rumours and counter-rumours swept the city. Char's main source of information was the surgeon: 'Dr. Leckie tells me many stories. People come to him all day long with all kinds of tales, & they seem to be getting very much alarmed for themselves, & there are projects & petitions for arming & drilling on all sides.' So bad did this rumour-mongering and prophesying become that Lord Canning finally introduced a bill to control the local press. This was immediately denounced as the 'Gagging Act' because although it was largely aimed at the Indian newspapers, who were the worst offenders, Canning had refused to discriminate between Indian and British papers. His attempt at even-handedness made the Governor-General the chief enemy of the British press both in India and England – and it did very little to curb people's fears.

The arrival of the 78th Highlanders in Calcutta was a signal for panic among certain sections of the Indian population fed by rumours that the Governor-General had 'sent for a regiment of demons who wear no clothes'. This was followed closely by what came to be known as 'Panic Sunday', 14 June, when it was put about that the sepoys of Barrackpore were marching on the city. Pandemonium ensued as large numbers of Europeans fled with their arms and their valuables to places of safety. In fact, their fears had not been entirely groundless. At half past one that Sunday morning one of General Hearsey's sons had arrived at

OPPOSITE Charlotte Canning dressed in her serge riding outfit and with argus pheasant plumes in her hat.

Government House with what was said to be positive information that a planned uprising of the entire Barrackpore Brigade was to take place within hours:

> There was an alarm of an intended rising last Sunday morning in the Barrackpore Brigade & the General of the Division sent notice of it to Lord Canning and proposed to assemble all the European forces near at hand and to disarm the whole native force & this was done that very day, the 78th Highlanders being very opportunely near Barrackpore. These very regiments I mentioned in my last letter to Your Majesty being amongst the best, we shall never know for certain if mischief was intended. But in such a time as this there can be no doubt that no precautions should be neglected & no warnings disregarded. The well disposed soldiers feel this measure sadly and are much inclined to desert.

Determined to set a good example, the Governor-General refused to have his Indian guards at Government House replaced by British soldiers. Char supported his stand. 'One cannot feel afraid here,' she insisted, 'where there are so few Sepoys and so many Europeans & where the ships are full of strong hearty sailors dying for a row.' But for all the show of confidence the good news, as British forces advanced up-country and had their first successful skirmishes with the mutineers, continued to be overshadowed by news of fresh disasters and more 'of the saddest messages from stations crying for help, where none can be given'. Allahabad, which for so long had appeared a bulwark against rebellion, suddenly collapsed:

> The sudden change of the horrid 6th regiment surpasses all we have heard of treachery. The officers believed it to be sound and staunch, & they indignantly contradicted anyone who said a word against it. The men all volunteered to go against Delhi: they had a letter of thanks from Government, & it was read at six on parade, & they went off giving three cheers for 'Company Bahadur'. Then there came a rumour of mutinous irregulars being expected along the road, & two companies & nine guns were sent down to the Bridge. About nine, some distant volleys were heard by the officers with these men, and the next moment they turned & fired on them. Some officers were killed & others got away, one by swimming the river. The officer who swam gave the alarm to some cavalry he believed to be staunch, & they started at once, but, after a few yards, shot their captain, a most excellent officer, believed to be much beloved. The first distant volleys proved to be from the cantonments, where the rebels fired at the whole of the twenty officers coming out from mess, & killed many of them, including the six poor young cadets who were on duty there on first joining.

Char had always done her best to 'mother' the young cadets of sixteen and seventeen when they first arrived in Calcutta and the deaths of these youngsters distressed her greatly:

Ensign Francis Chamier of the 34th Bengal Native Infantry, stationed at Barrackpore in February 1857. His regiment was disarmed and disbanded in April, six weeks after Sepoy Mangal Pande had run amok, wounding an English officer and sergeant-major and inciting his fellow sepoys to mutiny.

A poor little Raleigh, a quite young cadet, really a mere child, who dined with us lately, and whom they were laughing at because he looked tied to his sword, being so small, was killed as he rode away by himself from the cantonments. Another poor boy, recommended by Lady Mansfield, who dined with us the same day as John Hayter's son, is killed, shot down by that horrid 6th regiment.

Poor young Hayter was killed at Benares. He was doing duty with the 37th, still awaiting his regiment. He was shot through the body & both legs. It is very sad. I liked that young Hayter, & C. thought him pleasant & promising the day he dined with us two months ago. Poor fellow! He had better have remained a post-office clerk. A young MacNab, a cadet we knew, just joined, was killed at Meerut.

The horrors one hears daily are worse & worse, and as yet there is not a ray of sunshine in the gloom. We always say, 'When Delhi falls all will come right,' but this long delay tries people too hard. I have often tried to think 'the worst is over', but worse still comes.

Although Allahabad was quickly restored to British control by the timely arrival of Colonel Neill and an advance guard of his Fusiliers, more alarming accounts continued to come in from further up-country. Both Lucknow and Cawnpore (Kanpur, today) were besieged. In Lucknow Sir Henry Lawrence had long expected the worst and had prepared his Residency and the surrounding grounds for a long siege. However, the core of his garrison was made up of men of the 32nd

Foot, drawn from nearby Cawnpore, which had left that large military cantonment with only a token force to protect a number of sick and convalescent soldiers together with the wives and children of the 32nd Foot. Their fate was sealed when General Wheeler, in an act of quite incredible stupidity, chose to abandon a strong position beside the river for a totally exposed site in the military lines. 'It seems incredible that such a place could have been held a *day*', Char was later to write. 'They had no real shelter, were very far from the river; even the well was exposed, and water could only be got at night; the barrack roof at best was thatch, and it was gone, and the walls quite riddled. The trench was hardly a ditch – no depth at all; and the guns were left bare, without the least defence around them.' By 21 June their circumstances were beginning to cause grave concern:

> Cawnpore is now the most anxious position, but every one speaks alike of Sir Hugh Wheeler and his brave spirit. There is not a better soldier, & all say, if any one can hold it, he will. But all the civilians & women & children have taken refuge there, & he has very few troops even now. We know that the native troops have turned & left him, & fired the town, & he is shut up, & probably short of provisions, so there is great reason for anxiety, and it will be some time before he can be relieved from Allahabad, about 130 miles off.

Two days later the centenary of Plassey came and went. Despite rumours in the bazaar that Delhi had been retaken, there was nothing to be heard from that quarter. In Calcutta all the attention was focused on Cawnpore and Oude, with Neill and five hundred of his men pushing on alongside the Ganges as fast as they could go and a second column, under Brigadier Havelock, hurrying to reinforce them.

For some days there was no definite news to record. The rains had started and communications were worse than ever. 'I pass my days much as usual', wrote Char at this time, 'and often draw the fruits and flowers, & read all the India histories of former troubles like ours. What will Ld Dalhousie think of all that is happening here?' Char also reflected on her own position:

> I never wished the Governor-Generalship to be offered to C., & I think we did very happily at home, & I hated leaving all my own people & friends. But I did not at all object to leaving my monotonous London life, & I took great delight in all the novelty of impressions on coming to a new country; and, as far as I have been able to lay hands on information of things going on, I have been most exceedingly interested. Of late, it has been painful, & anxious, & terrible; but I do not know anything I should dislike more than to be told that C. would not have two or three or more years here, so that he might see India again prosperous, & on the way back to good order, though fifty years will not put it back into

the same state in which it was, so far as attempting to civilise & give liberty & our English ideas of blessings to the country.

On 26 June Lady Canning added two lines to the day's entry in her journal. How the news could have travelled so fast remains a mystery. 'There have been horrors in Cawnpore, if we must believe a native's story', she wrote. 'I think he exaggerates, so I will not repeat them.'

Pages from Lady Canning's journal: a fair copy was usually sent home on the mail steamer every fortnight.

CHAPTER V

'Remember Cawnpore'

THE first rumours that some frightful calamity had overwhelmed General Wheeler and all those with him at Cawnpore – some four hundred British soldiers and civilians and an equal number of women and children – were received in Calcutta with disbelief. Lady Canning found them impossible to take seriously – yet she could not dismiss the story out of hand: 'July 4. The mail goes off today, & with such a wish for good news to send, I have put off my letters till the last moment. Today it is a little better again, tho' a horrid report that Cawnpore has been abandoned, & Sir H. Wheeler & everybody massacred, came yesterday. Today it is not confirmed, & Col. Neill disbelieves it, though a native says he saw the Europeans trying to escape in boats & all killed.' Subsequent messages from Allahabad also spoke of a riverside massacre and of great loss of life – but these, too, were discounted. 'A great doubt seems to exist about Cawnpore', Char noted four days later. 'A great many people do not believe it.'

It must have come as something of a relief for her and for many other European women similarly placed when quite suddenly Calcutta began to be filled with refugees, mostly British wives and children brought down-river by the steamers. They nearly all needed to be housed, clothed and comforted – and here, at last, was an opportunity to take some active part in the conflict. Char and everyone in her household rose to the occasion:

> I have been making a collection of clothes to send to the houses of the destitute arrivals. Rain & West & my three tailors are working hard, & I have engaged four other tailors, so plenty of clothes can be made. Some of the poor ladies arrive in rags only, & others have merely a gown & nothing else. At last my large trousseau has turned to good account & is nearly expended.

Charlotte's kindly disposition also served her well as a succession of distressed ladies were brought to see her at Government House, each with a sad story to tell. 'We had a dinner of a few refugees in the evening', begins her account of one such encounter:

> The Lennoxes from Fyzabad & Mrs Webster from Banda, a very pretty young

> woman, who had travelled for a fortnight in a buggy, which was upset at the first start & broke her collar-bone. But on they went, sleeping under trees by the roadsides at night, & flying from place to place. Mrs Currie gave me a piteous account of the refugee people in the house she looks after – children with careworn anxious faces, who were obliged to lie in bed the first day, whilst their only garment was washed. Almost every one, in all their dreadful histories, has to tell of some kind Rajah or faithful servant, & now and then even of a sepoy. Poor Mrs Currie's nerves are very shaky. As she sat down to dinner, she said to her cavalier, 'I hope we shall rise safely from dinner'.

This same 'old Mrs Currie' also reported to Lady Canning that the 'nerves and minds' of many of those she was caring for were 'unhinged': 'She says the refugee women in many cases are most strange and odd. They show no feeling. One she had known from a child, had lost her husband, and fled, and she was full of her escape, and in high spirits. Another remembers nothing, but was found wandering with her children, in the jungle.' That this last refugee, Mrs Mills, should have remembered nothing was hardly surprising, considering what she and her two children had just come through:

> The girl is seven, the boy five – nice good little things, pale, but rather pretty and merry. Their mother was somehow left behind in Fyzabad. She was either stupid about not moving or not frightened, and the others waited in vain and went off without her. Her husband was away at the moment on duty, and killed. The sepoys came in and plundered the house, but finally sent her off with her two children in a boat. They wandered a fortnight from village to village, sometimes sitting all night by the river-side, with the wolves and jackals howling around, the little girl and her mother watching in turn. The child used to tell the villagers when they came near not to wake her mother. Once some Sepoys came, and the poor woman got up and said, 'Kill us all at once', but they simply turned away and left them. The child talks very simply about it, and said the villagers used to ask her to explain what her mama said to them. Probably the child pronounced much better, and was intelligible. This poor woman, besides dragging about the heavy child that could not yet walk, was about to have another. It was born dead.

In all the anxiety and turmoil the arrival of one of the wonders of the modern age in Calcutta passed almost unnoticed. 'At any other time, the first lighting of gas in India would have made a great sensation', Char noted in her journal on 5 July. 'It was done this evening, and a crowd of natives assembled at each lamp-post, the lamplighter hurrahing as the light flared up.' By mid-July the terrible news from Cawnpore had been confirmed. After three weeks of relentless battering Wheeler's garrison had been reduced to a pitiable condition. Taking

up Nana Sahib's offer of a safe conduct in boats away from Cawnpore, the survivors of the siege had made their way down to the water's edge at Satichaura Ghat – where their boats had been fired and all the men massacred. About 150 women and children had been spared. They and another fifty or so English women captives from the surrounding area had been imprisoned in a small bungalow known as the Bibighar.

The rescue of these women and children became the chief concern of the little army fighting its way north from Allahabad, now led by General Havelock, a 'wiry little old man, covered with medals'. Although he was derided by the Calcutta papers for his old-fashioned attitudes, the Cannings thought highly of him. 'No doubt he is fussy & tiresome,' Char had noted, 'but his little old stiff figure looks as active & fit for use as if he were made of steel. We believe he will do well.' But even Havelock's best efforts proved to be in vain. As his force approached the outskirts of Cawnpore, all the remaining hostages were put to the sword and their bodies thrown down a well.

It is reported that when news of this second massacre was conveyed to Charles Canning, he was quite unable to sleep and spent the night pacing his rooms, agonising over what he saw as his failure to prevent the tragedy. Charlotte herself was to admit that 'the horrors of Cawnpore haunt me'. Five days after the Bibighar massacre she sat down to explain the circumstances to the Queen:

> The sad news of the fall of Cawnpore after the sad death of Sir H. Wheeler and the massacre of the garrison has proved true but no details are known. The horror of the story is now redoubled by hearing that all the poor women and children in the Nana's hands were put to death on the approach of General Havelock. The advance of General Havelock's little army has been most gallant. It took some time to procure sufficient carriage for it but there was not an hour of unnecessary delay & it has advanced by the most rapid marches and defeated the enemy 3 times, taking 12 guns, 4 guns & 6 guns! I believe if it is possible without too much delay, the Nana will be again attacked at his own home at Bithor about 9 miles from Cawnpore. He is a small Rajah who used to pretend and delight in everything English and used to entertain the officers and go out shooting with them. The horrors committed by this man are too dreadful to relate. He has murdered every fugitive that passed thro' his country & his treachery & wickedness appear incredible.

With Cawnpore fallen all their anxieties were now focused on Lucknow and the British garrison besieged there. But from here, too, there was only bad news to report:

> The death of the brave Sir H. Wheeler is not the only one of your Generals that

> Your Majesty has now to lament, for I grieve to say that Sir Henry Lawrence has died of his wound. He received it in a sortie which failed thro' the treachery of his native artillerymen & cavalry & he had to retire into the fortified 'residency' & died soon after. He is a most dreadful loss. His defence of Lucknow had been so spirited & the worst of it so nearly over, that his death at such a moment seems doubly sad. There seems every reason to hope that General Havelock will arrive in time.

A fortnight later Char was able to provide more details of the events in Cawnpore:

> I cannot write to Your Majesty all the horrors we have to mourn over. The Cawnpore massacres were the worst of all & little has yet come to light. Two officers and two sergeants have been heard of who escaped from the boats by swimming & some drummers' families. Poor little scraps of journal, one by a child, & a letter from a lady to her mother with verses of 'Farewell' were picked up in that house where they were murdered. The sight of those rooms makes strong men faint – the bodies were never seen. All were already thrown down a well. I think the spot will be cleared & consecrated & a simple memorial put up to their memory. I hear of letters from a large party of merry happy girls there who at first thought Cawnpore 'so delightful'. 'They did not wish to be sent away, they feared nothing & the life was so pleasant, like a picnic every day'. After the siege began what a cruel contrast! Their house was shelled & the roof gone. Many were wounded. A list of deaths by wounds & cholera up to the last dreadful day was found & it has given comfort to many to see the names of their friends on it.

Although driven from Cawnpore, the rebels had gathered in great strength across the river, forcing Havelock's small force to fight for every mile of ground. 'But the thought of the crowd of helpless people & the brave little garrison of the Lucknow "residency" must urge him on', Char declared. This Residency was now the only part of Lucknow in the hands of the defenders. 'It is a large compound or garden surrounded by a low wall & I believe new entrenchments. There are several houses within it & one with large banquetting rooms. In one building Gen. Low made 3 underground rooms which are often used for coolness in the hot season. They are lighted with windows only 2 feet above the level of the soil. In these rooms, we are told, the woman & children are placed for safety.' There were four hundred and sixty of them all told, defended by rather less than twice that number of British and Indian troops.

Char had also to report the death of another general, Sir Henry Bernard, who had succeeded General Anson as commander of the still unsuccessful Delhi Field Force. 'They never seem to have thought it safe to assault & enter the town',

Unshipping elephants from Burma, a spectacle witnessed by Charlotte Canning who later set down an account of the spectacle in a letter to Queen Victoria: 'They were hoisted up from the mast & suspended by a bandage passed under their bodies & fastened to a hook, then a crane swung them round & lowered them to the water's edge. The great creatures sprawling in the air were more ridiculous than I can describe. Some however behaved with very good sense, steadying themselves by the bulwarks & rigging, other roared & struggled, but all walked off quietly ridden by their "mahout" driver as soon as they were released from their trappings.'

Char wrote, reflecting the widespread feeling in Calcutta that an assault on the rebel stronghold was long overdue. 'It is very large & very rich & there may be risk but the delay has been terrible. Nearly the whole sepoy army has rushed to Dehli [sic] & been beaten in detail but they continue to get in.'

The continuing failure of the authorities to regain the initiative from the rebels was beginning to have further repercussions. In Bengal fresh outbreaks of mutiny in hitherto loyal Indian regiments had to be put down while other regiments believed to be wavering were disbanded. To Lady Canning's distress it was decided that the Governor-General's own elite company of bodyguards, whom she had grown to admire and trust, would have to be disarmed. 'All have fought in our battles, & have medals', she protested. 'Some have 4, 7 and even 8 clasps, & many have belonged from generation to generation. The Subadhar-Major's relations were there in Warren Hastings' time, & one came in 1805. I do not want them to be affronted.' Nevertheless, as Char described to the Queen, 'General Grant

[Acting Commander in Chief] wished it & Lord Canning with regret agreed.' So the disarming went ahead:

> The time & manner of it & final order were yet to be given when an opportunity occurred that the officer in command, Major Thomson, could not neglect. When alone in the lines with the native officers he came in conversation upon the topic of disarming and they assured him the men would understand the motives for it & willingly give up their arms. He said, 'Then ask them to do it at once'. Carts were brought up & they put their swords & carbines and ammunition into them quite readily & stood at the doors without swords looking quite good humoured. It is right to be cautious. The fanatical mania comes so unexpectedly & frightfully. Major Homes's is a frightful story. He raised the 12th Irregulars (Cavalry) & loved them as his children. They were doing zealous service severely punishing offenders, keeping a district quiet, till the moment they hacked him & his wife to pieces.

The Cawnpore tragedy was the culmination of almost ten weeks of outrages and disasters so numerous as to leave the British community shattered, humiliated and clamouring for revenge. However, from early August onwards virtually every sea-going vessel that came up the Hooghly brought troops responding to the Governor-

British men-of-war and East Indiamen moored in the Hooghly at Calcutta, *c.* 1859. The vessel covered with canvas awnings on the right is the Governor-General's barge *Soonamookie*, in which Charlotte made several long journeys up and down the Ganges.

General's call for help. Lord Elgin arrived with a fleet of warships and 1700 fighting men, and a mail steamer delivered the new Commander in Chief, Sir Colin Campbell (later Lord Clyde), the most able of the Crimean War generals, who slowly began to put together his army of retribution. 'Our troops now begin to pour in. This is delightfully exciting!' Char could write in her journal in mid-September. 'The Mauritius, an enormous steamer, has the greater part of the 93rd Highlanders; the Adventure, which started a month before, has brought out part of the 23rd and 82nd; the Belgrave and another bring Madras troops, and the Belleisle has some men of the Highlanders & 82nd. The Fort church on Sunday morning was full of the tidiest men, in little brown holland short blouses, with red cuffs & collars, & white cap covers, showing they were sent out well provided for the climate.'

Although the fate of the Lucknow defenders still hung in the balance – 'our agony is for Lucknow' – and Delhi had still to be recaptured, the critical stage of the war appeared to be over. 'Now there is far more hope than fear', Char informed the Queen on 10 September. For the first time since April she felt able to go out to Barrackpore again, perhaps to clear a head that for weeks had been full 'day & night of fighting, & guns, & murders, & counting up marches & roads & distances'. To her delight Charlotte found gardeners and workmen laying out the improvements that she had planned, 'some simplifying of patterns and widening of walls in the garden, a great many groups of plants with brilliant flowers near the pools & tanks, & above all, the new terrace – most successful. Only the foundations & piers of the balustrade are finished, but it looks beautiful.' The

Lady Canning's newly laid out terrace at Barrackpore; a pen and ink sketch made at high tide during the Rains of 1859 when the work had been completed.

only note of discord was to be found in the menagerie: 'I enquired after the lovely blue bird, like the one in the fairy tale, and found he was dead, & stuffed, & in the Asiatic Museum. Sure enough I had recognised him the other day, & had promised Lord Elgin the sight of one exactly like him, only alive.'

Less than a month later, on 26 September, Lady Canning returned to Barrackpore with Sir Colin Campbell as her guest. It was to be the happiest day she had spent for months:

> We settled to be off at six. The morning broke with torrents of rain, but they happily ceased and we had a cool pleasant drive. Sir Colin talked all the way, telling no end of military stories. When he grows very indignant, he pulls off his little cap, & scratches his head violently, leaving his hair standing bolt upright, exactly like his portrait in Punch. He was charmed with Barrackpore, and certainly it did look most beautifully green. We had a short walk through the garden on the way to the house, and a general overlooking of my improvements, which are still in the rough.

After breakfast the Commander in Chief was taken across the river to visit Sir John Hearsey and inspect the troops. As Char sat on the verandah watching the erection of the new balustrades on the terrace, a telegram arrived addressed to 'Lady Canning and Sir Colin Campbell':

> I knew it must be good news, & it was: 'Delhi has fallen! Our troops entered by the breach on the 14th.' To hear this at last, after longing for it after so many

EVERY INCH A SOLDIER.

PAM (BOOTS AT THE BRITISH LION). "HERE'S YOUR HOT WATER, SIR.
SIR COLIN. "ALL RIGHT. I'VE BEEN READY A LONG TIME."

Sir Colin Campbell (Lord Clyde) prepares to embark for India. A *Punch* cartoon showing the Crimean War hero with Lord Palmerston.

> months, seemed scarcely possible to be real. An ADC came soon after with the whole message, in which 'our loss severe', is the worst part, but it must always be so in an assault and fighting in the streets. Sir Colin came back from the cantonments in the highest spirits, having given the news to be spread everywhere! We could think of nothing but this great news, and I settled to go back to Calcutta as soon as possible after the sun was lower.

Before that Char took a walk by herself through what she had come to regard as her own private garden:

> It was a grey pleasant day, and I ventured out a little with an umbrella, under the great banyan & about some walks – a thing I had never done at that hour before. I was well repaid. The whole place was alive with the most gorgeous butterflies, of all sizes, & colours, & shapes. The orchids in the banyan are in brilliant health, and I am only sorry to think that, except for a day at a time, we shall have no enjoyment of that charming spot. As the elephants were at the door long before the carriage, we got upon them for a ride to the park gate. Punch would have made a nice vignette of Sir Colin with me in a howdah on the top of an elephant, talking over our great news in the greatest delight.

More cheering tidings awaited their return in Calcutta. The rebels were in flight in Delhi and Havelock's forces had at last broken through the city walls at Lucknow. The Residency was about to be relieved. Now all the talk was of the restoration of British rule – and of revenge. 'The number of offenders to be brought out & punished is fearful to think of & it will be long before that dreadful task ceases', Char warned the Queen. 'There is great exasperation felt by many against all who have brown skins. We cannot be much astonished after the horrors that have occurred.' Privately, in her journal, she expressed her fears more strongly: 'There is a spirit of revenge abroad which is dreadful. I always say, "Let us be severe and punish, but not unjustly, and above all, let us be as unlike these monsters as possible, and not copy them." But the things people say they would like to do, would be quite as bad as the acts of the Nana.' Already in Cawnpore and Allahabad Neill and his men had begun to translate words into deeds. With 'Remember Cawnpore' as their rallying cry they were exacting vengeance with relentless brutality – and they were far from being the only offenders. 'The bloodthirsty feeling of Europeans is most distressing', wrote Char in her journal on 5 September, after hearing that British soldiers in Dinapore had taken the law into their own hands:

> I believe all sense of justice is gone from many. The horrid story of the murder of some of the Sepoys who laid down their arms at Dinapore and did not mutiny,

is palliated in the newspapers, & they think it too much punishment that the whole [British] regiment has to answer hourly roll-calls, as the real offenders are not discovered. The story is a mystery, but screams were heard in the night, & many Sepoys and women found killed. I feel not only horror at such a crime, but a most painful addition of disgrace, in thinking of it as committed by our own soldiers, & countrymen, & Christians.

But Dinapore was unusual only in that the reprisals were publicised. In many other places the killing went unnoticed by the outside world. 'There has been no leniency as yet', Char recorded on 12 September, citing an example:

Only imagine, 80 executions in one village being unreported & only mentioned incidentally in a private letter from one man to another! Hanging for plunder and burning villages has been most common. Sepoys deserve the severest punishment, but as every Sepoy cannot be hanged or blown from a gun, it becomes expedient, as well as just, to discriminate a little, and punish with death those of the regiments who killed their officers & did other horrible crimes, and not every man, without enquiry, who is caught slinking away to his home.

It was precisely to limit these excesses that the Governor-General had circulated a minute that was to earn him the name 'Clemency Canning', intended as a label of opprobrium. In one of Canning's infrequent letters to Queen Victoria, dated 25 September, he explained why he had thought it necessary to issue this minute:

There is a rabid and indiscriminate vindictiveness abroad even among many who ought to set a better example, which it is impossible to contemplate without something like a feeling of shame for one's fellow-countrymen. Not one man in ten seems to think that the hanging and shooting of 40 or 50,000 Mutineers besides other Rebels, can be otherwise than practi-

THE CLEMENCY OF CANNING.

GOVERNOR-GENERAL. "WELL, THEN, THEY SHAN'T BLOW HIM FROM NASTY GUNS; BUT HE MUST PROMISE TO BE A GOOD LITTLE SEPOY."

The *Punch* cartoon of 24 October 1857 epitomised a widespread belief that the Governor-General was being too lenient in dealing with the mutineers.

> cable and right – nor does it occur to those who talk and write most upon the matter that for the Sovereign of England to hold and govern India without employing – and, to a great degree, trusting – natives, both in civil and military service, is simply impossible.

His 'clemency' resolution offered no mercy to known or even suspected rebels. Its main purpose was to draw a distinction between the real mutineers in the army and the many sepoys who had played no part in the uprising. It insisted that wherever order had to be restored the law should be administered 'with such promptitude and severity as will strike terror into the minds of the evil-disposed', but that the punishment of crimes thereafter should be 'regulated with discrimination'. It was this apparent leniency that aroused such fury among the Governor-General's many critics, who saw it as further evidence of Lord Canning's weakness. He was accused of being indifferent to the sufferings of the victims of the rebellion, of exciting contempt for the Government of India, of putting Indians before his own countrymen. 'The great outcry here, especially in newspapers, is that brown faces are preferred to white', Char noted with resignation, 'and that they are petted and indulged, and Government will not listen to anything said against them.'

Even after the passing of the 'Gagging Act' in June the English-language press had kept up a constant stream against the Governor-General and his senior advisers of what Char described as 'mischievous, contemptuous, and silly writing, with the favourite epithet of "cowardly imbecility" repeated over and over again'. Much of what was said could be laughed off, such as the 'absurd stories against our old khansumah – a sort of maître d'hôtel. One says he has been plotting and run away, another that he is a Thug. He was handing me a cup of tea as I was reading one of the articles.' But some of the attacks carried more serious implications and when it was put about that there was a serious rift between Sir Colin Campbell and her husband, Char made sure that the Queen got to know the truth of the matter: 'I am sometimes amused as well as provoked to see the pains taken by foolish & spiteful newspapers to try to establish that the Gov. Gen. & Comm. in Chief are at variance upon all sorts of subjects, when nothing can be further from the truth.' Though she made light of such charges, Char's constant references to them illustrate that she was well-aware how damaging they were to her husband's reputation. Nor was this her only preoccupation. While she scarcely commented upon her own health – other than the odd passing reference to 'a touch of fever' – all her letters and notes express concern for her husband and the strain that he was undergoing. 'C. looks daily more worn and bleached', reads one such entry made during this trying period. 'I think it will be well for him when he can get fresher air and peace of mind.'

Nothing can have done more for Lord Canning's peace of mind than the Queen's unwavering expressions of support. The long letter sent from Balmoral in the second week of September was written just after Queen Victoria had received the details of the Bibighar massacre by the mid-August mail steamer:

Dear Lady Canning,
That our thoughts are almost solely occupied with India & with the fearful state in which everything there is – that we feel as we did during Crimean days & indeed far more anxiety, you will easily believe. That my heart bleeds for the horrors that have been committed by people once so gentle – (who seem to be seized with some awful mad fanaticism) on my poor Country Women & their innocent little children – you, dearest Lady Canning who have shared my sorrows and anxieties for my beloved suffering Troops will comprehend. It haunts me day & night. You will let all who have escaped & suffered & all who have lost dear ones in so dreadful a manner know of my sympathy; – you cannot say too much. A Woman & above all a Wife & Mother can only too well enter into the agonies gone thro' of the massacres. I ask not for details, I could not bear to hear more, but of those who have escaped I should like to hear as much about as you can tell me.

I feel for you & Lord Canning most deeply! What a fearful time for you both, but what a comfort for Lord Canning to have such a wife as he has in you, calm, and pious & full of trust in Him who will not forsake those who call on Him. The distance & the length of time between the Mails is very trying & must be harrowing to those who have (& who has not amongst the gentry & middle Classes in England – Great Britain I should say?) relations in uncertain & dangerous places?

The retribution will be a fearful one, but I hope & trust that our Officers & Men will show the difference between Christian & Mussulmen & Hindoo – by sparing the old men, women & children. Any retribution on these I should deeply deprecate for then indeed how could we expect any respect or esteem for us in future?

Those Troops (Native) who have remained faithful deserve every reward & praise for their position must be very trying & difficult. The accounts of faithfulness & devotion on the part of servants are also touching & gratifying. I cannot say how sad I am to think of all this blood shed in a country which seemed so prosperous – so improving & for which, as well as for its inhabitants, I felt so great an interest. We are not desponding – but we are very very anxious to impress the Government here with the immense necessity of providing a sufficient Reserve of Troops to feed those sent out – & to prepare for the worst –

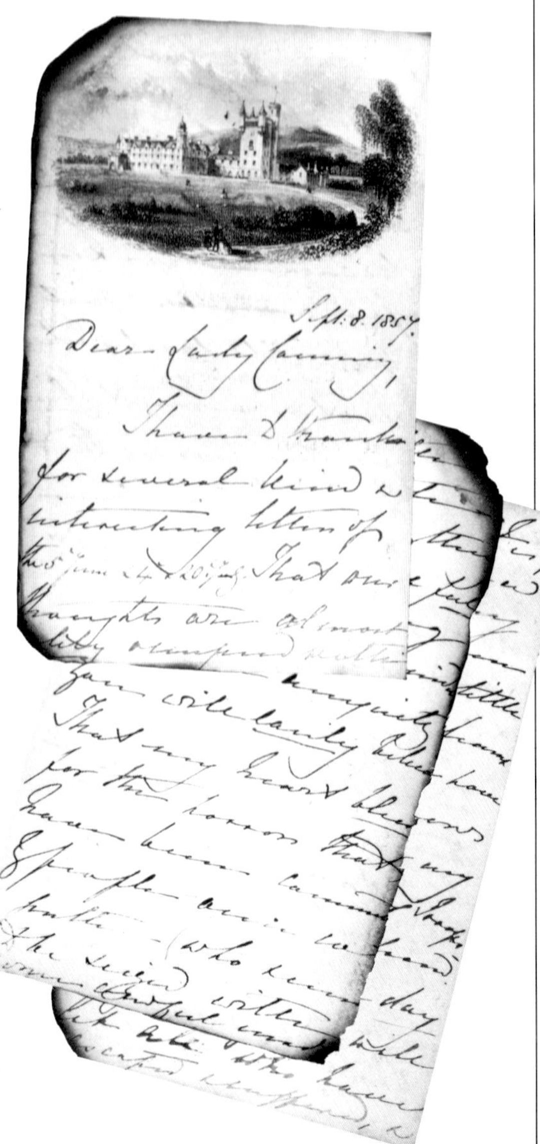
Sept: 8. 1857.
Dear Lady Canning,

The first pages of Queen Victoria's letter of 8 September 1857, containing her reactions to news of the first British losses in the uprising.

& Lord Canning may rely on our urging this unceasingly, for without it – I am sure, we cannot hold India.

God bless you, dear Lady Canning – we have great confidence in Lord Canning and wish him all possible success in his arduous task.

Ever your's affectionately V R

Such an expression of sympathy – even if it was not received in India until mid-October – was welcomed with 'great delight' by Lady Canning. 'I believe that Lord Canning will himself express the gratitude he feels for Your Majesty's gracious words expressing your confidence in him', she replied. 'I well know how cheering and encouraging it is to him in all his difficult and heavy duties & cares to be assured of such support.' Knowing that a petition calling for Lord Canning's dismissal had just been drawn up by a number of Calcutta citizens and sent to the Queen, Char was anxious to have the contents of the letter as widely known as possible. 'I shall take care that all I can reach may know of your Majesty's kindness', she assured the Queen, adding in her journal that 'it is such a pity I cannot be indiscreet enough to copy and hand it about; it would please people so much'.

A second letter, equally full of understanding and, if anything, even warmer in its support, arrived six weeks later. In it the Queen set out her own thoughts on the vexed question of what exactly constituted just retribution and how it should be effected – but perhaps its real significance was that it was written just when Lord Canning's 'clemency' resolution was being given a second mauling by the British newspapers. As the British Government and Parliament prepared to pass judgement over the events of the summer of 1857, the Cannings took comfort in the knowledge that they could hardly have found a better ally:

Windsor Castle
October 22nd 1857

Dear Lady Canning,
I cannot tell you how thankful I am for your writing to me so regularly by every mail or what a pleasure & satisfaction it is to me to receive your letters which (without flattery) are universally considered as the best which are received from India, & I hope you will continue writing to me by every mail as long as Affairs are not restored to what they were, before this dreadful mutiny.

Thank God – the accounts are much more cheering & those of Lucknow are a very great relief. The continued arrival of Troops will I trust be of great use, & that no further mutinies

& atrocities will take place. As regards the latter I should be very thankful if you & Lord Canning could ascertain how far these are true. Of course the mere murdering – (I mean shooting or stabbing) innocent women & children is very shocking in itself – but in civil War this will happen, indeed I fear that many of the awful insults &c. to poor children & women are the inevitable accompaniments of such a state of things. Some of these stories certainly are untrue – as for instance that of Colonel & Mrs Farquarson who were said to be sawn asunder and has turned out to be a sheer invention, no such people existing in India! What I wish to know is whether there is any reliable evidence of eye witnesses – of horrors, like people having to eat their children's flesh – & other unspeakable & dreadful atrocities which I could not write? Or do these not rest on Native intelligence & witnesses whom one cannot believe implicitly. So many fugitives have arrived at Calcutta that I'm sure you could find out to a great extent how this really is.

I am delighted to hear that that most loyal excellent veteran Hero Sir Colin Campbell is well & that you like him; I was sure you would, for it is impossible not to do so – & we never for a moment credited the shameful lies of disagreement between him & Lord Canning. If he is still with you say everything most kind to him. I am glad to hear that he does not share that indiscriminate dislike of all brown skins which is very unjust – for the Inhabitants have, it appears, taken no part in this purely Military Revolution – & while summary punishment must alas! be dealt out to the mutinous sepoys – I trust he will see that great forbearance is shown towards the innocent & that women & children will not be touched by Christian soldiers. I hope also that some rule may be laid down as to Ladies in future living in such an unprotected way as they have done in many of those stations & that at the first alarm they will be sent away to places of security, for really they must be dreadfully in the way & it must be so paralysing to the Officers & Men if they have their wives & children in danger. Sir Colin talked to us of the bad system of 'Bungalows' when he was going to start for India.

As I write to you & Lord Canning is so busy I will not write to him also & beg you to communicate what I have said to you to him. He may be sure of my warmest support & approbation.

Now with the Prince's kind remembrance (he is as you will imagine much occupied with India) – to yourself & our's to Lord Canning believe me ever,

Yours affectionately V R

I send you some photographs of Balmoral & Osborne which I think will interest you.

CHAPTER VI

'Lucknow Is Saved'

The restoration of British government in India was a laborious, ugly business that dragged on through the Cold Weather months of 1857 and well into the start of the following Hot Weather. When Delhi fell, the bulk of its sepoy garrison escaped to join one or other of the many rebel strongholds in the Gangetic basin above Allahabad. Large numbers made their way to Lucknow, bringing up the numbers laying siege to Havelock's reinforcements and the original defenders of the Residency to sixty thousand men. Others assembled under the banner of Nana Sahib outside Cawnpore. Not until late October did the Commander in Chief decide that his numbers were sufficient to take on the enemy.

Sir Colin Campbell reached Allahabad on 1 November but not without incident, as Char related to the Queen:

> He & his staff were quietly travelling in their little carriages, when they suddenly came in sight of two companies of the mutineers of the 32nd. 500 yards off hastily crossing the road. Sir Colin himself counted 12 elephants & 25 horsemen with them – those very elephants he had so much regretted when the news of this latest mutiny came & he was in such want of every beast of burden. He is described as sitting on the top of his carriage spying at his enemies & quite unwilling to turn back. At last the whole party did turn back one stage & they kept with some of the 82nd regiment who were travelling up by bullock train.

This mode of transportation had now been organised into as efficient a system as the means allowed: 'The bullock-train has carried 250 since the beginning of the month, counting officers. In 13 days it reaches Allahabad: so a whole regiment arrives there in 60 days. They have four men in each bullock-carriage, & two walk in their turn, so six belong to each carriage. The commissariat is now said to be in excellent order on the road, & there are fixed stations where the men feed & rest.'

OPPOSITE The Battle March; the score sheet of a musical composition apparently written to celebrate the fighting on 14 September 1857 when British (and Indian) troops in four columns stormed the city of Delhi and recaptured it from the rebels.

THE BATTLE MARCH.

DESCRIPTIVE OF
THE TRIUMPHANT ENTRY INTO DELHI
Arranged For the
PIANO FORTE
BY
JOHN PRIDHAM.

What was not working so well was the telegraph system – and for all sorts of bizarre reasons: 'The telegraph wire is now cut up into slugs by the insurgents', reads one short entry in Lady Canning's journal. 'It is as thick as iron rod, because the monkeys used to swing on it, & break common wire.' But rebels and monkeys were not the only hazards:

> They often have stoppages from posts being blown down or little chance accidents. But once the telegraph stopped, & no one could discover why. At last they found a web of one of the gigantic spiders, which connected the wire with one of the lightning conductors, & carried the message into the ground, instead of along the line. The spiders' webs had been known to make double wires useless as they connected them so often.

Even after Havelock's departure many hundreds of troops remained billeted or camped in Calcutta, putting a severe strain on the city's hospitality. The wild behaviour of the Highlanders and the sailors, in particular, made them objects of fear among the Indian population. According to one report that Lady Canning passed on to the Queen, the Navy's Jack Tars were said to be '4 feet high & 4 feet round & carried 9 pounders & 12 pounders in their arms as a cooly does a parcel', while the Highlanders 'count still as fiends kept in cages & let out to fight'. One night Char was woken by shouting in the street outside Government House: 'I did not imagine anything had happened, & now I hear five sailors killed a policeman & wounded another. These native policemen must run great risk, & often tremble amongst the drunken sailors & soldiers in the streets.' Char reckoned that 'the sun and the spirits' was a dangerous combination – and her views were shared by many:

> There is a great outcry in Calcutta, and for once a reasonable one, against the grog-shops, & the danger of them to the British soldiers & sailors. The spirit is bad, & very cheap indeed, & they have indulged terribly in it. Some got so drunk that their medals were robbed from them, & a few have died of drink. I am sorry to say the Highlanders have been by far the worst. A good many days ago, the Lieutenant-Governor [of Bengal] was told to enforce the Act withdrawing licences from those shops where people came out drunk, but now a better thing is being done by establishing a Government canteen on the Maidan in tents, where good spirits & tea, & coffee & beer can be had, & skittles & games, & newspapers & books for amusement. The officers, to carry out this order, all came to C. for instructions.

The Calcutta Maidan was also the setting for the presentation of colours to the newly raised Calcutta Volunteers on 20 October. This was a rare opportunity

for Lady Canning herself to perform a public duty and she relished the challenge, however modestly she described the affair to the Queen:

> I must tell your Majesty of a humble military spectacle in which I bore a part. I am afraid the photographic representations are not successful enough to send. It was to present colours to the Calcutta Volunteer Infantry and Cavalry. I gave them on horseback reciting my speech not very correctly I am afraid but few heard! Sir Colin was much pleased with the little corps & the pains every man took to do his very best. There are about 600 Infantry 180 Cavalry & 4 guns – and the privates are gentlemen & clerks & shopkeepers – English & East Indian (which is the polite term for half caste). My cortege would have been brilliant enough for Your Majesty for I had 5 Generals & staffs in attendance – Sir Colin, Gen. Mansfield, Gen Wyndham, Gen Garrett & Gen Low, the member of council. I am told 20000 people were present & the moral effect of this little force being seen is supposed to be very good.

To her mother Char confessed that her rendering of the speech, which she and Lord Dunkellin had worked on together, had been 'very awful!'. She had begun bravely enough but 'after the first two lines I felt I was in for it & away went the words out of my head & I stammered a second. Then happily I remembered the second part & it ended well. I think not more than five people knew how badly I did it, I don't think the rest could hear but I shouted it out as loud as I could.'

Another service that Char was able to perform was visiting the wounded troops, a number of whom had been brought down-river from Cawnpore in towed barges known as flats:

> Most of them are in the Fever Hospital attached to the Medical College – a wing is given up to them & they are in large wards of a height very superior to anything of the kind in England. Lord Canning & I went to see them & found them comfortable & well cared for & rather surprised at some comforts such as mosquito curtains at night. It put me so in mind of former visits with Your Majesty to the wounded men [of the Crimean War] but there are some differences too. Sunstroke is as common as frost-bite [was] in those wards. It looks much less bad but I suppose it is very dangerous. They say numbers are knocked down by it. In those first marches in Oude & at Bithur it was dreadful & in short the sufferings of the sick & wounded in that expedition were quite fearful.
>
> I have found several doctors who were in the Bosphorus Hospital & friendly to the nurses. There are none here. Their office for many reasons would be rather different but I dare say if not so useful the soldiers would like to see them.

As well as offering comfort to the wounded, the needs of the refugees still had

to be attended to. Dr Leckie was the chief co-ordinator of this relief effort with Lady Canning playing a useful supportive role. 'A good many women and children are already gone to England', Char was able to inform the Queen on 23 October:

> Their passages being paid wholly or in part and a small sum left in hand to take them to their friends. Here a good deal has been done in the way of giving clothing & loans supporting persons in homes of refuge, 11 in number. A great many are supported by the Fund in other places. I still think we do not know the full amount of distress. We know that in those districts where the mutinies broke out all the officers & civilians had to fly with mainly the clothes on their backs & lost all; but merchants & planters & contractors also must have lost all their works & buildings & no subscriptions or compensation can reach them. There will also be many refugees from Oude & those parts when the road to the North West is open.

The fund for the refugees had been opened in June. Both the Cannings had set an example by making substantial donations – Charlotte was not surprised to find that in the English papers she was reported to have given a thousand pounds when the actual sum was a hundred – and there had been a generous response in Britain as well as in India, both in cash and kind: 'Four enormous boxes of gifts of clothing have come to my care. All Salisbury contributes, & Southampton, & a Mr. Allen of Clapham, & Jay of Regent Street – a chest full of beautiful pieces of muslin and alpaca, & camelite & ribbon etc. I hand them over to committees, & advise a good quantity to be sent up at once, by a lucky opportunity there is, to Allahabad, to meet the Lucknow refugees.'

Once Sir Colin Campbell had reached Cawnpore it was only a matter of days before Lucknow was again assaulted by a British force and the Residency's occupants – after an epic eighty-seven-day siege – relieved and evacuated. Char was able to give the Queen the good news on 25 November: 'This time we may really trust that the garrison is safe, for we hear not only of Sir Colin's meeting with Sir James Outram & General Havelock, but that he has safely deposited all those much tried women & children with the wounded in the rear of his force. It will be a great comfort to know of them safe across the Ganges, & still better to see them arrive here!'

These glad tidings reached the Queen at Windsor the day before Christmas, provoking an ecstatic response: 'Thank God! Lucknow is saved, & the poor, unhappy Ladies, Women, Children & sick at last after so many months agonies of doubt – safe! I cannot tell you how truly thankful we all are, & how rejoiced it should have been known just before Christmas!' In fact, the rejoicing was premature. The defenders could not be immediately evacuated and their rescue

had been bought at very high cost. Among the many dead was old General Havelock, 'worn out in mind and body', who was accorded a handsome private obituary in Char's journal:

> I knew him better almost than any one, and used to try and keep him in good-humour when he seemed a little inclined to be affronted. He was very small, & upright, & stiff, very white & grey, & really like an iron ramrod. He always dined in his sword, & made his son do the same. He wore more medals than I ever saw on any one, and it was a joke that he looked as if he carried all his money round his neck. It is curious now to remember how his appointment was abused here, when he was called 'an old fossil dug up, and only fit to be turned into pipeclay'.

'The Campbells are Coming: Lucknow September 1857'; an engraving of the popular painting by F. Goodall portraying a supposed incident of the epic siege when a young woman claimed she could hear the bagpipes of General Havelock's relieving force of Highlanders, Sikhs and Madras Fusiliers.

The actual withdrawal from Lucknow turned out to be a protracted affair. Rebel troops overran a British force guarding Sir Colin Campbell's rear at Cawnpore and the Commander in Chief found himself having to engage the enemy on several fronts. The news of the progress of the Lucknow evacuees had to be conveyed to the Queen stage by stage. On 11 December Char could write of their arrival at Allahabad: 'Sir Colin was obliged to be disencumbered of the long sad procession of 4 miles of women & wounded before he could strike his blow. When they were gone to Allahabad he marched upon the enemy in the town & defeated them completely taking 16 guns & baggage & pursuing them 14 miles.' On Christmas Eve there was little progress to report, although plenty of incident:

Only one steamer with a flat in tow, & the women & a large number of wounded soldiers is yet on its way down. The river is very low & 4 other steamers with the 'flats' (great covered boats) were heard of aground on sandbanks. A few gentlemen of the garrison have come here by the road and I have heard from them the most interesting stories of the terrible months of the siege. They still have a gaunt hungry look & anxious expressions. The Principal of the Martiniere School was one of them. I think there were 70 boys at Lucknow, some of the elder were drilled & fought & kept watch – the others worked & the younger ones fanned the sick and wounded in Hospital. Children died in numbers and nearly every one had scurvy. The women & children were very much shut up in the 'Pyelkhana' or underground rooms & one can well understand now in so many letters people speaking of the delight of once more being in the open air.

The faithfulness of the sepoys in the garrison will always be one of the most

'Thank God! Lucknow is *saved!* Queen Victoria's emotional reaction to the news that the women and children in the Residency were being evacuated.

> astounding passages of the Mutiny. They used to talk to their former comrades across the street and ask after their own families. The commonest question was to know who commanded them but to this they never got an answer.

At last, on 9 January the first steamer arrived with its flat in tow – to be met by a stirring welcome:

> A Royal salute has just been fired and the ships in the river are all dressed to welcome the landing of the first of the Lucknow Heroes and Heroines, 15 poor widows & 20 wounded officers & 130 men. The first widow walking on shore with her 4 little children was loudly cheered & so they were all. So many were received into friends' houses that few required the lodgings prepared by the Committee. The officers have a large airy house fitted up for them & the men have one of the Orphans' Schools & will be under Your Majesty's army surgeons.

In contrast to the men, the women from Lucknow turned out to be 'strangely well':

> They lived in small parties together & hardly ever went out of their doors & were so busy with their children & their household work that they hardly knew the full extent of their peril & the present moment was engrossing to them. The men knew all but too well, and the look of fatigue & anxiety tells on them. I must not forget however that only those who are wounded or ill are here and the others on active service.
>
> Poor Mrs Cowper is the only one I have heard of who never got used to the sound of the firing. The others all say they were quite accustomed to it & many say the silence when it stopped was awful & they always began to think of mines, their greatest terror. It is touching to hear of a baby [of] 2 years when it heard the evening gun at Calcutta [fired at six p.m.] asking 'Mama is everybody killed'. Shot & bullets were the poor little things' playthings.

Char also met one of the real heroines of the siege, Mrs Polehampton: 'From the 1st day to the last of the siege, she worked in the hospital, beginning with her husband, the Chaplain, & not ceasing even for a time when he died. She was only lately married & is very young. Her clear calm face so fresh & fine reminds me of one of the soeurs de charité one so often sees with that same expression.' This young woman was most anxious to accompany the wounded on their passage home, which Lady Canning arranged for her. 'I hear how delighted they were to see their friend Mrs Polehampton come on board', she was able to write later. 'I could not omit giving her a letter to Miss Nightingale for they [are] right to

(TOP LEFT) The three youngest daughters of Mr Ommanny, the Judicial Commissioner of Lucknow, and their governess. The girls appear to have survived the fighting although their father was killed by 'a round shot to the head'. (TOP RIGHT) Captain Adolphus Orr of the Oude Military Police Corps with Mrs Orr and her sister. They and their daughter survived a massacre of Europeans at Aurangabad but were found hiding in the jungle and brought to Lucknow – where Captain Orr and other male prisoners were shot. Mrs Orr and her girl were held captive in the Kaiser Bagh palace for five months before being smuggled out of the city and taken to the British camp. (RIGHT) Mr and Mrs George Couper both survived the siege. 'I had Mrs Edmonstone with Mrs Couper from Lucknow to luncheon,' wrote Charlotte in her journal on 2 February 1858. 'Mrs Couper is the wife of the young civilian [civil officer] so praised in the despatches. She is very timid & quiet, but has become robust & tolerably strong-minded. She never could get used to the sound of a gun, but lost all her fear of cholera & small-pox, & at times there were cases close to her. She was shaken in her bed by the springing of a mine the very day her child was born! She seems to have fared very ill for food, & had to save all her little store of arrowroot & sugar for her children.'

Casualties and survivors of the seige of Lucknow; their photographs were found, together with those of many other Europeans and Indians, in two albums among the ruins of the Residency at Lucknow. Both volumes were sold for a large sum and later acquired by the war correspondent of *The Times*, W. H. Russell.

know each other – tho' this gentle young creature thinks herself not to be compared to her.'

Lady Canning and Florence Nightingale were old friends. In 1853, as chair of a London women's hospital committee, Char had taken the controversial decision of appointing Miss Nightingale as its superintendent. She had also helped select Miss Nightingale's nurses for the Crimea. She knew her worth but, as she told the Queen, she did not see what Miss Nightingale could do in India: 'Miss Nightingale writes that she is ready to serve here & if there is work "in her line of business" she would start at 24 hours notice. I am sure her offer is hearty & true, but it would be wrong to encourage her to come.' It was Char's belief that 'three months hence there will probably be little fighting except perhaps with the different columns marching over the country.' But here her judgement was at fault. It took another three months just to clear the mutineers out of Lucknow and another full year before the last rebel force was finally broken up.

Even before the fate of the Lucknow defenders had finally been settled Char had become deeply embroiled in an enquiry to establish exactly the manner and the degree to which victims of the various killings had suffered. This was partly in response to the Queen's request but also because Char was determined on her own and her husband's account to reach the truth that lay obscured behind all the distortions that had been spread abroad and accepted as certain fact: 'People on the spot say the stories going about are not true of that place but happened elsewhere, and so on. Those who have gone from place to place never find evidence of the horrible treatment everyone here believes.' The subject of what was delicately referred to as the 'ill-usage' of women clearly held a deep and morbid fascination for both Queen Victoria and Lady Canning as, indeed, it did for their Victorian contemporaries, but it has to be remembered that what had just happened in India to their community was something quite outside the British experience. Its nearest parallel was Cromwell's butchery of Catholics in Ireland two centuries earlier. 'Your Majesty was anxious to know on what evidence the worst stories of horrors & ill treatment of English women were founded', Char wrote on 9 January:

> I am now able to send a few extracts of letters on this subject. Lord Canning desired his Private Secretary to write to the authorities in many places to enquire confidentially into this painful matter. Evidence might have come out of the truth, so it was asked for privately. The result is the very reverse, & shows that slaughter & extermination seem to have been in all cases, the object of the mutineers & there is not a particle of credible evidence of the poor women having been 'ill used' anywhere. The only approach to it in the papers received was the mention of the 'boasts of a mutineer' at his execution – & they were not believed. Your

Majesty may read of an inscription found on the wall of the house at Cawnpore & that seems to have been a forgery & not there when the house was carefully examined in July on Gen Havelock's first arrival. One can not have imagined a hoax possible in such a spot, had there not been many inscriptions of some foolish persons placed there since.

I am not sure how much of this evidence (if it can be so called) will be made public. It was asked for confidentially & it ought to be clear & conclusive or it may bring down a controversy likely to do more harm than good by stirring the subject – but still the gross misstatements must be contradicted for absurd as they are they obtain credit from many persons. The horror of the massacres cannot be exaggerated & the dreadful mutilations & insults perpetrated upon dead bodies have given rise to most of the dreadful stories. When one thinks in what a happy peaceful state of things the massacres first occurred, where there had been no fighting to exasperate, no injury to revenge, it seems as if demons had possessed those men. It will always be a mystery of horror.

Charles Canning, meanwhile, had become increasingly frustrated by the problems of communication that his administration faced in Calcutta. The city of Allahabad, lying midway between Delhi and Calcutta, struck him as being a more suitable base from which to govern the country and oversee the conduct of the war. In late November he informed Char of his intention to move up-country as soon as the Commander in Chief had secured his position in Cawnpore. He would be going alone, with only the minimum of staff. Although distressed by his decision, Char put a brave face on it for the Queen:

Lord Canning has been always looking forward to the time when his presence here should not be absolutely essential, & that he could go up towards the North West Provinces, where he has much to do. He has settled to go to Benares & Allahabad almost immediately. I am afraid it will be 2 or 3 months before I get leave to follow him, for as he is very severe in prohibiting other persons from taking their wives & putting them 'in the

The Baillie Guard Gate, Lucknow, where General Havelock and his men first joined up with the besieged forces in the Residency on the evening of 25 September 1857, ending the siege of eighty-seven days.

The Alumbagh, occupied by Sir James Outram between the first relief and the final lifting of the siege of Lucknow; one of the many scenes of battle visited by the Cannings during their tour of the city in October 1859. General Havelock was buried nearby.

> way' I am bound to give a good, rather than a bad example, & must be left behind.

However, there was to be some compensation for this separation: 'I expect my cousin Colonel Charles Stuart & his wife in a very short time which will be a great comfort to me. He is to succeed Dunkellin as Military Secretary when he has to go home to attend Parliament.'

Charles and Minny Stuart arrived in Calcutta in time to spend Christmas with the Cannings at Government House. Both were to leave lively accounts of what they saw and experienced. 'Bowing red men with joined hands awaited us at the door', wrote Mrs Stuart, describing her arrival at Government House. 'Then we were ushered up to the drawing-room, and there in clear muslin was a thin, slight, pale Lady Sahib, with eyes gleaming with welcome! She did indeed receive us with heartfelt cordiality and affection. Lord Canning came upstairs to our top-of-the-house apartment to see me, and after he went down, Char stayed and talked and talked, and kept saying, "You must be so tired, but don't send me away. I have not talked like this for ages".'

There was no mistaking Lady Canning's joy to be with close friends again. 'It is so delightful to see the real pleasure and comfort which it gives to dear Charlotte to have us here', noted her cousin:

> Her manner to everybody is perfect – really enchanting. At the large dinner-parties, of which there have been several since our arrival, she goes about and speaks to everybody in a charming way that I have never seen in any viceregal or colonial court. The Governor-General does his honours extremely well too, but he is in general very silent. I do not think the A.D.C.s help much: there are four of them, and as all their names begin with B, they have been called the B flats.

For all the Governor-General's taciturn ways, Colonel Stuart was greatly impressed by his strength of character. He found it 'impossible not to feel respect and admiration when talking to a man who had faced such astounding difficulties and dangers with such serene courage, and, regardless of abuse and calumny, coldly and ineptly supported by Government at home, had been resolute, through good report or evil, to do his duty firmly and uprightly, and with as much humanity as justice and prudence would allow. He said the only thing which really vexed him was the lies circulating regarding his intercourse with Sir Colin Campbell.'

What did worry the Stuarts were the long hours that Lord Canning spent at his desk and the effect this was having on his health: 'He is not looking well, is very tired, and fearfully overworked', was Minny Stuart's comment. 'The intensity and quantity of his present business can scarcely be imagined. After the last mail he suddenly sank from exhaustion, and was some time in rallying. Dr. Leckie says it was fatigue of the brain: he had neglected his breakfast, and had written till eyesight failed and he could not see anything.'

Despite all the pressures of work, the last days of 1857 were passed very cheerfully at Government House and Char was in good spirits when she wrote to her mother describing their Christmas activities:

> They try here to keep Christmas in English fashion, but I think they have rather a dim recollection of it. The shops dress up and illuminate, and people crowd there to buy plum-cakes, which they call 'Christmas Cakes', and all sorts of knick-knacks for presents. The natives call it our 'great day', and to show how they understand our customs, we all find hot-cross buns at breakfast. After church we found the whole of the servants paraded and drawn up, with all the peacocks'

fans and flappers and signs of dignity, and the head-servant croaked a sort of speech. The Stuarts were highly amused at this specimen of manners and customs.

People are all hospitable on Christmas Day, and collect together all the forlorn and young students and cadets into sort of family parties. We had all the belongings of the household, including body-guard, and played a game of commerce for prizes.

No one in the Governor-General's household stayed up to see the New Year in: 'The old year finished by waking us all out of our first sleep by a gun and ringing of bells, & letting off rockets, & every possible noise. They "salute the happy morn", not only of Christmas, but of the New Year also, with 21 guns.' Char celebrated New Year's Day by going to church and attending a fête given for the children of the British troops. 'It was a cheerful day,' she recorded, 'for I never felt more glad of the end of any year than of the last terrible and unhappy one.'

The Jumma Masjid, Lucknow's main mosque, painted by Charlotte Canning in October 1859.

CHAPTER VII

'A Glimpse of the Burning Plain'

On 30 January the Governor-General left Calcutta for Allahabad, accompanied by his doctor, two of his ADCs and his new Military Secretary. 'Of our sad leave-taking this morning the less said the better', noted Colonel Stuart. 'Dr. Leckie tells me that Charlotte was in private quite upset, but she was her grand self when she came to the door of the great drawing room.'

Soon after their departure Char informed the Queen that she did not expect to be able to join her husband for a 'very long time'. Accordingly, she had made arrangements to spend the Hot Weather in the Nilgiri Hills in South India: 'I believe Commodore Watson is likely to give me a passage in the Chesapeake the end of this month or the beginning of March & I shall go for two months into the Nilgherries & allow myself one month in the way.' It was a sign of the vastly improved state of affairs that she could begin her next letter to the Queen, written on 23 February, by remarking that 'I do not think since last May I have ever had so little to write to your Majesty'. However, she was able to speculate at length about the marriage of the Princess Royal that had just taken place in England, before ending her letter with the comment that 'All is profoundly dull & quiet here'.

Queen Victoria, meanwhile, was by her own admission 'entirely engrossed with the preparations for & festivities of the marriage of our dear Child, as I may say I still am with her sad departure'. Proudly she reported that 'Victoria looked extremely well – & behaved beautifully. We spent one very happy week with the dear young people after their marriage which seems to me (as it will to you) a dream, & it is only 18 years ago – on the 10th – that I was married!' But the Queen also confided in her former lady-in-waiting her distress at seeing her eldest child leave home: 'Alas! The departure was a dreadful day & our poor Child was quite heartbroken, at leaving us & her dear Home & Country. She has left a sad blank.' Photographs of the 'young couple' were to follow very shortly, together with 'a piece of Wedding Cake & of the trimmings of Victoria's Dress'. In all the excitement, the troubles of the Indian Mutiny were almost – but not quite – forgotten. 'What our poor Sex have had to endure', was the Queen's final

comment on the safe arrival of the Lucknow women in Calcutta. 'What courage & resignation they have shown!'

Charlotte sailed for Madras on board the *Chesapeake* on 8 March. With her went her two maids, Rain and West, Minny Stuart and two ADCs, Major Bowie and a young man whom Char was always to refer to in her letters as 'little' Johnny Stanley – the newest and youngest addition to the Governor-General's staff. A younger son of Lord Stanley of Alderley, the Hon. Johnny Stanley had been expelled from Harrow at fourteen for foul language and wild behaviour (such as jumping over the headmaster's table at dinner). At seventeen he had gone out to the Crimea with the Guards, only to be invalided home within a month, and he was still in poor health when sent out to India three years later. Arriving with the *Chesapeake* in January, he had very soon established himself as a 'very merry young ADC'. Lady Canning found him a delightful character, 'like a merry page, so civil & useful', while Johnny Stanley for his part was to become Char's most devoted admirer.

Johnny wrote frequently to his parents during his two years in India and these schoolboy letters of his, unpunctuated, full of passionate likes and dislikes, give an inside view of the Cannings and their circle quite unlike any other. He delighted in shocking his parents with wild, racist remarks. 'My beau idée is to shoot niggers in action & just to have a little blood on my sword', he declared soon after his arrival – an ambition that, to his evident regret, was never realised. Instead of soldiering, he found himself sharing the 'dreadful task' with Major Bowie of attending to Lady Canning and Mrs Stuart – the 'widows', as he first referred to them. The former he judged to be 'a cosmopolitan with a leaning to Windsor Castle' who 'never employs the ADCs on anything but the house work', but he was quick to perceive her good nature. 'Lady Canning is so kind', he was writing a month after his arrival. 'She never says an unkind thing of anyone tho' she must notice many things, she is so very quick & her memory is wonderful.' Lord Canning began well, in Johnny's estimation, but soon proved a disappointment: 'Lord Canning never opens his mouth all day even at dinner.' However, after the Governor-General's departure for Allahabad it was Char's companion, Mrs Stuart, who became the chief object of Johnny Stanley's scorn: 'Now Mrs Stuart lays herself out to please in that peculiar manner one might perhaps call toadying. She is besides inclined to domineer over the staff & fancies one is there to wait on her. I may say this as she makes up to me in order to impart her unkind observations & also to have an ally in the enemy's camp.' Over the next few months this dislike of the unfortunate Mrs Stuart ripened into a loathing that was quite possibly mutual. 'We are usually a silent set,' Mrs Stuart was to write in one of her letters home, 'easily daunted except that dauntless boy J. Stanley of whom we get far

more than is good for himself, though Char spoils him at one time, scolds him at another & thinks she keeps him in order.'

Char's ill-matched little party reached Madras after a pleasant voyage in the *Chesapeake*. 'She steamed down against the wind in five days', Char wrote to the Queen on her arrival:

> I was disappointed not to see that fine ship under sail but I had a pleasant time with the amusing sight of man of war evolutions of the crew & I lived most comfortably in the cabins the Commodore gave up to me – Lord Harris came on board to take us all on shore & we landed thro' a surf not much greater than most days on the Brighton Beach. The Chesapeake went on in a few hours to Trincomalee to try to save the treasures wrecked on the Ava. I believe very little was at first saved of 250,000 £. It was sad that so many of the poor ladies from Lucknow & wounded officers were in that wreck & had that new terror & again left with only the clothes on their backs.

Also lost on the *Ava* were a number of Lady Canning's and Johnny Stanley's letters home, the latter commenting: 'How infernally provoking they have gone & lost the Ava off Trincomalee & all the mails I don't care a straw about the ship but all my letters, I wrote such a quantity.' Some were recovered, including Char's letter of 9 February to the Queen, which was eventually delivered blotched but still legible.

After a brief stay in Madras, where Char found it strange to see armed sepoys once again, the party started off into the interior of the Indian peninsula, first by train as far as Vellore and then transferring to carriages. Moving by night to avoid the heat, Lady Canning and Mrs Stuart slept stretched out on cushions in what had formerly been Mrs Anson's travelling coach. Three uncomfortable, dusty nights on the road, moving at an estimated eight miles an hour and changing horses every five miles, brought them to Bangalore where they were greeted by the Commissioner, General Sir Mark Cubbon. 'The most grand seigneur old man I almost ever saw' was Char's impression of him – and not without reason. The General had never left India since first setting foot in the country as a fifteen-year-old cadet in 1800 and for the last quarter of a century had ruled the Mysore region with a rod of iron. 'The old general is most remarkable', Char told the Queen. 'He has the most perfect manners & is a very fine looking man & yet he has been 58 years in India. He has a store of most interesting recollections & can give information in the most agreeable manner & is as alive to all that goes on in Europe as if he had but just left it.' Sir Mark Cubbon had arranged for them to spend several days at his mountain villa, spectacularly sited on the summit of a local hillfort, Nandydroog, which jutted almost two thousand feet out of the surround-

LEFT The branch of a forest tree found only in the Nilghiri Hills, *Gordonia Obtusa*, known locally as *negetta*.
RIGHT The *Calliandra Haematocephala* 'pink powder-puff' flower.

LEFT Nutmeg, coffee and tea seeds, described as being 'from a spice garden of Mr Thomas, a collector, Coonoor Ghat 1000 feet above the plains'.
RIGHT The branches of a casuarina tree, introduced to Bengal from New South Wales.

'A glimpse of the burning plain'; looking south from 'Lady Canning's Seat', Coonoor. 'Sketched the plains on a fine evening,' noted Char in her journal on 7 May, 'the colours glowing, and the tanks [artificial ponds] full, like little lines of silver in all directions; hills miles & miles away, like distant coasts, a 100 miles off at least'.

ABOVE A Hindu temple and bathing tank (probably Parathasarathy temple) on the southern outskirts of Madras.

Lady Canning's white pony with *syce* (groom). After her death the pony became the property of her friend, Emily Bayley.

ing plain. The ladies were carried up in *tonjons*, accurately described by Mrs Stuart as 'the bodies of Bath-chairs with hoods, carried on a palanquin-pole. Eight bearers carry you, crooning a most painful song all the time; and a man, one shade superior, walks by you with a cane, to thwack them if they stumble or squabble.' Char found the air at 4800 feet above sea level deliciously cool and fresh: 'There is a panoramic view of enormous extent but the hill itself is full of beautiful subjects, rock & trees & tanks & buildings – wild & full of monkeys & leopards & other wild animals.'

To reach the Nilgiris from Bangalore the travellers had to pass through the city of Mysore, where the Maharaja was determined to entertain the Governor-General's consort in style:

> The Rajah of Mysore exerted himself to the utmost to do me honour notwithstanding my announcement of wishing to travel very quietly. I was met by a burst of shrieking music & the road lined with the most quaint soldiers & Elephants & Camels & horses caparisoned & standard bearers with gilt devices reminding one more of the procession of the Prodigo than anything real. All this was still more wonderfully repeated on my departure, & men ran beside the Carriage holding umbrellas, & fly flappers & twirling a sort of silk mantle before me. The little old man paid me a visit & most loyal speeches were interpreted, always ending with a 'refrain' that he owed all to the Govt. – & as he drove off he begged the resident or agent (I do not know the exact title) to mention again that no Rajah in India was in the same position as himself owing all to the Company & that when it sorrowed he sorrowed & when it rejoiced he rejoiced. Notwithstanding all this many people think he knew of plots as well as his neighbours & would have willingly availed himself of an opportunity to do mischief. His direct government was I think taken away by Ld Wm Bentinck [Governor-General 1828–35] when it was found to be much abused. His family was that vanquished by Hyder Ali & singled out & returned when Tippoo [Tipu Sultan, killed at Srirangapatnam by the British in 1799] was defeated. I imagine the little old man wished me to speak well of him & his attentions were very amusing. I was offered carriages & horses, his band thrice a day, & dinner with 100 dishes came, & those curious garlands of flowers & tinsel arrived repeatedly, & even were sent 10 miles after me.

This account of her meeting with the Maharaja of Mysore formed part of Char's letter to Queen Victoria written a week after her arrival at their final destination, the tiny hill station of Coonoor, built on the edge of the southern escarpment of the Nilgiri Hills:

> I arrived in these hills a week ago and find the climate delightful, neither hot nor cold & I can wear warm clothing & light a wood fire in the evening & sit

The irrepressible Johnny Stanley surrounded by other members of Lord Canning's military staff. The photograph was taken (by Charlotte Canning, perhaps) in the Viceroy's Camp at Fatehgur in November 1859. Also in the picture is the Military Secretary, Major Sir Edward Campbell (on right) and the mild-mannered Captain Jones (seated on left).

out of doors amongst orange trees and green house flowers. To reach such an atmosphere after enduring 90 degrees Fahrenheit (about 16 hours before) at Mysore was most delightful. The plains below are high & the heat barely lasts 3 months but it is at its worst now & I felt it more than at Calcutta, for the houses are not shut up & are furnished with thick carpets & no punkahs – & ice cannot penetrate so far inland.

I have a cluster of tiny cottages covered with roses in a beautiful garden with a view across the valley of hills with woods of evergreen & rocky precipices – they are about 6000 ft above the plain & whenever they approach the drop down into it they are of great beauty – but the character is of gigantic hills & not mountains – I have a glimpse of the burning plain but enough to remind one of what I have left.

The main hill station in the Nilgiri Hills was Ootacamund, one of the first hill sanatoria to be established by the British in India (in 1821) and reckoned by many to be the 'Queen of Hill Stations'. Lady Canning, however, had merely passed through it. Three years earlier Major Bowie had accompanied Lord Dalhousie to the Nilgiris and at his suggestion they chose to stay at the quieter hill resort of Coonoor, twelve miles further south. Mrs Stuart and Johnny Stanley gave rather different accounts of this last stage of their journey. The former describes Lady Canning setting off 'brisk and well' at 5 a.m. on a hill pony, while she followed in a *tonjon*:

> I travelled on and on for miles very comfortably, through a most picturesque but entirely solitary country, and it was only just at last that I began to think it was very lonely, and that my eight dark and speechless friends (or foes?) had it to ourselves for weal or woe! The clatter of little Stanley's pony as he came galloping to see after me was not unwelcome, and then we entered and travelled along the most picturesque ravine imaginable! and arrived at this fairy bower of a place.

Johnny Stanley, however, saw himself as victim rather than rescuer: 'Mrs Stuart is so nervous riding & so afraid I shall leave her, that she asks me to smoke knowing I cannot then go on with Lady C. She gives every horse she gets onto a sore back.' This little squib was soon followed by stronger invective as Mrs Stuart's manner began to grate on Johnny: 'I do not like to abuse but Mrs Stuart is very tiresome; frequently indeed she is more civil to me than Lady Canning who scolds me so severely & kindly whenever I am naughty & I never can feel but pleased, whereas if Mrs S. opens her mouth on anything I say, all the blood of Charlemagne rises up in a jiffy.'

The party was now settled in a series of bungalows grouped together. 'Char and Rain and the drawing-room and dining-room are in one,' explained Mrs Stuart in a letter to Char's mother, Lady Stuart de Rothesay. 'West and I are in another; the two A.D.C's in a third, and our cloud of red and gold men in a village of huts just beyond. Char sketches, and I try to do so, a great deal.' Minny Stuart seems to have been quite put out by Lady Canning's revived energy: 'Char's genuine love of plants and flowers makes every step in the country of interest to her. She walks, to everyone's astonishment, up and down no end of steep hills.' This intense interest in her surroundings was well portrayed in Char's account of a day's ramble recorded in her journal on 5 May:

> After a rainy middle of the day, we went out, carrying a great tin box, to search for ferns. A slippery path took us down a woody glen, where we gathered eight

> varieties, and went on & on & down & down by zigzags into another glen, to a beautiful walk I had never seen before. The larger stream was fuller of water and of great beauty. By the side of it I saw the Hedychium growing wild, but rather of a creamy white variety, and a pretty Begonia on a great rock, for once within reach. The sides of this valley, down which the ghat [pass] road descends, are clothed with magnificent wood, but a great deal is being cleared away for coffee plantations. One spot is quite lovely. A long rickety wooden bridge crosses the stream which comes down from the Coonoor bazaar, falling over enormous granite boulders and great cliffs covered all around with trees. I never saw more gorgeous foliage, and a tangle of creepers, sometimes like curtains of great green leaves looped up with coils of ropes, binding the trees together, unlike anything in Europe. A few great black monkeys, jumping from branch to branch, relieve these spots delightfully. The stems of the trees are nearly all white, and a great many have bright pink or red young shoots or leaves.
>
> We came back by a very humble little burying ground of white tombs, with wooden crosses peeping out of the fern, where the Roman Catholic native Christians are buried. There are a good many, and I sometimes see the little polished brown children, with nothing on, but a little silver cross round their necks.

A favourite spot for Char's sketching – still known to this day as 'Lady Canning's Seat' – was on the edge of a steep bluff overlooking the deepest of the gorges cutting into the escarpment. Opposite, on the summit of a high promontory, was another of Tipu Sultan's ruined hillforts, known as Tiger Rock Fort, from which he was reputed to have hurled prisoners to their death. From here Char could gaze out across the endless expanse of that 'burning plain', resembling a 'blue sea with island, & here & there streaks of pink & blue & yellow all melted together, like the colours of an opal'.

Despite his thirst for violent adventure, Johnny Stanley enjoyed these excursions. 'Johnny's spirits never flag as you may easily believe & he enlivens our little party more than I can say', Char wrote to reassure his mother. 'I do not know what I should have done without such a merry pleasant companion in all my rambles & scrambles in the hills!' The young man soon became as avid a plant and flower collector as Lady Canning, assembling his own specimens to send home to his mother. Later Char was to declare that 'our wild little Johnny Stanley became the best collector possible, and knew them as well as I did, and would go to any distance to find them. I think his mother will be surprised when she unpacks his collection: it is exactly like mine, and he did it all himself.'

Johnny's devotion did not please Mrs Stuart, and two months after their arrival in Coonoor Johnny was writing to his mother with more complaints: 'Mrs Stuart complained to Bowie that I never spoke to her now & other silly lamentations

so he very properly told her she must have offended me in some way. She is absurdly jealous when I show my preference for Lady Canning – of course I like walking with her, she walks like a goat while Mrs S. puffs & blows & requires lifting over stones 1 ft high.' Poor Mrs Stuart was much happier indoors, where her more orthodox Victorian accomplishments could be shown to advantage: 'We have a pianoforte, a poor one, but on which I manage to play Beethoven', she wrote soon after arriving in Coonoor. 'I am not allowed to play these glorious sonatas at home, where they are thought dull, so that I am now enjoying a real treat in finding them appreciated.' Minny Stuart also sang, well enough for Char to observe later that it was 'one of our great pleasures. Her voice sounded always so round, & mellow & right, when others were so doubtful.' Johnny Stanley, naturally, was not among her admirers. 'I nearly went into a fit last night', he informed his mother in one of his letters. 'Old Mrs Stuart was singing "Peace be around thee", I had to go outside to laugh', adding in another letter that Mrs Stuart

Tree ferns at Coonoor, 5 April 1858.

Mrs Minny Stuart (seated) and Johnny Stanley together with a Mrs D'Aguilar. Probably taken in Coonoor by Lady Canning.

'sometimes begins to sing as if she was a merry young milk maid in a field – but that I always stop'.

What Lady Canning made of this comic rivalry can only be guessed at but she obviously enjoyed mothering the bumptious young Stanley. 'I never saw such an affectionate creature', she remarked in one of her several letters to Lady Stanley. 'You will not have disapproved of his being sent upon the easy quiet & humdrum duty of spending the hot months wholesomely in these hills. You will like to know that Mrs Stuart & I watch over him as if we were his grandmothers.'

Much as Lady Canning enjoyed her invigorating surroundings in the Nilgiri Hills, she was far from content. Writing to the Queen on 19 May, she intimated that she would not be happy until once more reunited with her husband. 'I hope very much he will find room for me, and let me join him when I can go up the river in the Rains', she stated plaintively, 'I am very impatient to return even to Calcutta for it is so painful to be so far out of the reach of letters, knowing so little of what passes in these anxious times. There is a daily post but Allahabad is 14 days off at the very least.' Her anxieties were well-founded because her unfortunate husband was now being assailed by a second onslaught of criticism, most

of it emanating from England where a new government had taken office under Lord Derby. Now it was being said that the Governor-General, from being too soft on the rebels, had gone to the other extreme.

As soon as Lucknow had been recaptured in March, Canning had ordered the release of what came to be known as the Oude Proclamation. Its purpose was to secure the immediate submission of the powerful landowning *taluqdars* of Oude by threatening to confiscate their properties. To the chief critic of the Proclamation in England, Lord Ellenborough, the newly-appointed President of the Board of Control, this seemed to be the very reverse of clemency: 'Other conquerors have, with a generous policy, extended their clemency to the great body of the people. You have acted upon a different principle; you have reserved a few as deserving of special favour, and you have struck, with what they feel as the severest of punishment, the mass of the inhabitants of the country.' This was the central charge laid against the Governor-General in what was supposed to be a secret despatch, dated 19 April 1858.

Ellenborough's intemperate despatch, published in full in *The Times* on 8 May, reached the Governor-General in Allahabad some three weeks later – just after Lord Canning had been struck down by a serious bout of fever. The severity of

Coonoor Ghat, June 1858, the road leading down from the Nighiri hills to the plains.

the illness was kept from Char by Dr Leckie, but her growing fears for her husband as he faced this new barrage of attacks, were impossible to conceal. 'For worry she is looking far less well than I had hoped she would on her return', noted Mrs Stuart as they started out from Coonoor on their return journey. Not until the party had reached Bangalore on 26 June, where a large bundle of mail was waiting for them, did Char know for certain that her fears were groundless. Her husband was well again, Lord Derby's government was supporting the Oude Proclamation and Lord Ellenborough had been forced to resign. What Char had to say in her journal during this trying period is not known but a letter written to a close friend in England, Emily Lady Sydney, conveys the tenor of her feelings very well:

> I have only just heard from C. since all the excitement on the publication of the Secret Despatch became known to him. He seems never to have doubted or hesitated for an instant as to the course he should take, & I am delighted to find it is exactly what I hoped it would be. You will find that he writes home defending his Proclamation, and that he remains here, carrying out the same policy he has held hitherto, and leaves it to Government to recall him, and send out some one else, if they are not pleased.
>
> How curiously people seem to have forgotten that almost the whole Sepoy army from generation to generation has had its home in Oude, and that any show of weakness or undue conciliation there would affect the very people we are unanimous in saying deserve most punishment. The great landowners, if they submit, will have their lands given back to them at once. They certainly are amply satisfied with the Proclamation, and would have been amazed at easier terms: for instance, I heard yesterday of 13 rebel zemindars who came to offer their submission on promise of their lives!
>
> You cannot imagine the joy with which I left those charming hills and that cool climate. Enjoyable as it was, it became nearly unbearable, from the impossibility of knowing what C. was doing in all this complication of troubles. The telegraph too was useless, and I could not ask him what I wanted so much to know, without putting all the clerks into my confidence. It is very odd that enemies and detractors should accuse him, of all men, of being vacillating and weak, when I believe he is one of the very few people who see their line of conduct so straight and clear, that such events as these hardly shake him at all, and he has gone steadily on without altering his policy in the smallest degree, however much the public cry has varied both here and in England.

Lady Canning might have been expected to convey very similar sentiments to her most powerful ally, the Queen, but her removal from the centre of events and the lapse of time made it difficult for her to put her husband's case in quite the same way as she had done earlier. When she next wrote, on 16 July, Char commented only indirectly on events that were already becoming past history

'Temples in thousands, like lace-work of stone, &, near the river, the slope covered with these most extraordinary & picturesque buildings & immense flights of steps'. The Nepalese Temple and the Lalita Ghat (steps) at Benares. If Lady Canning observed the Nepalese Temple's notorious erotic carvings she was far too polite to make any reference to them in her writings.

– while leaving the Queen in no doubt that 'clemency' was still at the forefront of her husband's policy: 'I believe Lord Canning is satisfied that the time is near, when it will be politic as well as merciful to extend a free pardon to large numbers of sepoys – indeed to all the less guilty men. I know that he is well aware such a step will raise a howl of indignation all over India, but it is his conviction that such a step must be taken if the country is to have real quiet.'

In fact, Queen Victoria had already made it plain to all concerned that she shared Lord Canning's views. Lord Ellenborough's failure to submit his controversial despatch to her before sending it off had caused much royal displeasure. Writing to Lady Canning on 1 July, she explained how very awkward her own position had been: 'The fact was I hardly knew how to write to you at that painful & distressing moment now more than six weeks ago, when things happened which I could not prevent & which distressed me more than I can say.' Her faith in the Governor-General remained unshaken:

> You know, dearest Lady Canning, what I always have felt about Lord Canning, & you will believe that these feelings are unaltered. I only hope that Lord Canning will not think of leaving his post or mind what has passed & there is but one feeling now about him here. People are very strange here, about six months ago the blood thirsting was too horrible & really quite shameful! Now that these disquieting early details have been found to be almost all inventions – they turn into the other extreme! All this came from judging things at a distance, & not understanding them & not waiting for explanations.

In the prevailing circumstances it was not surprising that Char provided the Queen with only the briefest account of her last weeks in Coonoor and the return journey to Calcutta. It was left to Mrs Stuart to pass on an account of what was undoubtedly the high spot of their last days in the south. On the outward journey Lady Canning had resisted the entreaties of the Maharaja of Mysore to visit his palace, but on the return leg she had (on Lord Canning's advice) relented – only to find herself playing a 'disagreeably prominent' part in the evening's entertainment. 'The pretext was a great tamasha [noisy spectacle] of horsemanship', was how Mrs Stuart described it to Lady Stuart de Rothesay:

> Char did it admirably, but I think she was half-frightened (if she knows such a word) when she found herself alone, as it were, the object of such a scene. The

OPPOSITE The Governor-General's state barge alongside the landing-stage at Morsheadabad, with the imposing Nizamat Kila, the palace of the Nawab Nizam of Morsheadabad, overlooking the river.

The 'small rather shabby house' at Allahabad where the Cannings were reunited in August 1858, a classic up-country bungalow of the early nineteenth century.

> crowds of eager faces and eyes, the torches blazing and glaring, the shrieks of the music, and the howls of praise and welcome, made us feel like actors in the 'Arabian Nights'. We drove through ranks upon ranks, with symbols and banners of all kinds of form and device, into the square of the palace, which was full of people, and elephants, and fireworks, to all of which clatter the horses were happily blind and deaf. Then the Rajah met Char. and taking her hand in a gold tissue handkerchief, led her daintily along – her graceful figure and his queer little body by her side being a sight to see. She was seated on a sofa, and the Rajah showered roses and orange-flowers upon her and at her feet, and we – gentlemen and ladies in attendance – had necklaces and bracelets of jasmine and tuberoses put upon us. After we had sat awhile in walked a Nautch [female dancer], very graceful in movements. This done, we were led to the Zenana [women's quarters]. The gentlemen took us to the door, and the Rajah alone went in with us. The passages were crowded with women. Before a rich portière, we were received by what must have been a really lovely woman, with good manners, covered with jewels and gold cloth. All the others, wives and not wives, daughters-in-law etc, seemed like mere bundles of gold brocade, rolling up, one after another to shake hands with Char.

Once more installed in Government House, Charlotte Canning professed herself to be 'quite enchanted to have got back to Calcutta, to the hottest July ever known, the sky of inky tint, and an atmosphere like a wash-house. Every one compliments me on my stout looks, and every one who has stayed looks parboiled.' Now she had only to wait for the river to rise in the wake of the monsoon rains, making it navigable to larger craft. Soon she was able to pass on the good news to the Queen: 'I hope in ten days time to embark on the river to join Lord Canning. My boat will be towed by a steamer with troops, & I ought to arrive in almost 3 weeks in Allahabad. I shall be very glad to join him, after 6 months absence at a time when he has had unusual cares and intensely hard work. He has hardly ever been able to spare more than a few moments now & then to write to me & I am now more than ever anxious to be again with him.'

Lady Canning would be accompanied, as before, by Mrs Stuart and the two ADCs. It was little Johnny Stanley, writing to his mother, who had the last word before they began their journey up the Ganges:

> Lady C. looked so very pretty tonight, in black for her grandmother, she is so kind to me but I wish she was not so silly & obstinate about going to Allahabad. Ld. C. wrote to her that the country was so unsettled she must not come up now. I do not at all like the risk for her, if the niggers find it out the brutes are sure to bring a gun down for practice. I will call them niggers & the name is too good for them.
>
> Mrs S. is getting more grumpy than ever.

CHAPTER VIII

'A New Order of Things'

It took the steamer towing the Governor-General's 'yacht' *Soonamookie* very nearly a month to cover the six hundred miles of winding, fast-flowing river between Calcutta and Allahabad. Even Lady Canning, 'one of the few people who always thrive in a monotonous life on board ship', confessed to finding the going 'rather tedious', and the 'sound of the constant rush of water rather wearing'. Nevertheless, she and her entourage travelled in comfort on what was really a large barge fitted out with a drawing-room, dining-room, five cabins and five bathrooms, and supported by the usual accompaniment of attendants who served them by day and 'spread their beds on the upper deck' by night. A second barge served as a cook boat, 'with servants & a farmyard on board', towing behind a third boat used for getting to and from the shore. For their protection the steamer carried on board forty English soldiers and three cannon. However, as Char reported to the Queen on her arrival at Allahabad, their services were not required: 'We passed the disturbed districts unmolested & there the people seemed to be tilling the ground & driving their cattle as usual, but I observed them to be all armed with long sticks. I thought twice that we saw villages occupied by the rebels, but they proved to be Seik [Sikh] piquets, in one case placed there because a steamer had been fired at a week before.' The riverscape, for the most part, was monotonously uniform: 'The banks are flat except in very few parts near the Rajmahal hills & the Fort of Chunar. Almost everywhere they are green and well wooded and the numerous villages and abundant herds of cattle look most prosperous.' To break the tedium of the voyage they made halts at several stations on the river:

> At Morsheadabad [Murshidabad] the Nawab Nazim came on board to pay me a visit. He has been one of the best behaved native princes in the late troubles. At Patna I arrived on the day of the Moharrum [Muslim festival] & saw very little, for I could not drive about & encounter the processions & the Opium Factory had given its workmen the usual holiday. 3 millions & ½ worth of opium, however, were shewn to me. At Dinapore & Berhampore I saw scenes of the mutiny, at Ghazeepoor 400 horses of the stud. 250 of these turned loose into a

field to gallop about, was one of the most beautiful sights I ever saw. But the great sight of all was Benares – one afternoon I spent in the civil station & outskirts & the next morning made an expedition thru' the Hindoo city. I now feel really to have seen India. Not a trace or touch of anything European exists there. Sounds, sights, & smells are all wholely & entirely Hindoo as they would have been 200 years ago. We were carried in silver tonjons or chairs thru' narrow alleys paved with flags between high carved stone houses interspersed with temples & trees. The great temple with its offerings all wet with Ganges water, & its domes covered with sheets of gold is a curious & horrible sight with its nearly naked painted priests and Faquirs but the main thing is the river's bank clustered with temples & flights of steps to the water crowded with gaily dressed bathers in the most holy spots of the sacred river. The present Commissioner is successful in deporting to a neighbouring jungle numbers of Braminee Bulls who used to herd about & be a nuisance & turn to every one & I saw very few of them.

Johnny Stanley, however, was not one for sights. In a letter written on board the *Soonamookie* on 7 August he reminded his parents that he had been away for

The Governor-General's 'yacht' *Soonamookie* and its steamer. The location may well have been the old East India Company trading settlement of Berhampore, just south of Morsheadabad.

The riverside temples and bathing ghats (steps) at Benares, August 1858.

almost a year and felt 'very old sometimes. Bowie says I am getting darker & my nose larger. I often think if I come back of what I will do to make amends for all my previous naughtiness.' His parents had admonished him for his anti-Indian remarks and his unkind attitude towards Mrs Stuart – but Johnny was unrepentant:

> I have no doubt you write for the best but if anyone else had written this of the Hindoos I sh'd have laughed. Ill treatment does improve them, plain talking does not & it is no joke trying to argue them out of their superstitions.
>
> Mrs Stuart would drive Papa mad in a week. It is coming too strong to tell me what sort of a person Mrs Stuart is. A woman is not universally disliked by all the men about her unless she deserves it. What do I care if she was a maid of honour [To Queen Victoria] it proves nothing, besides no one could help knowing it, she keeps Honble before her name even now & was absurd enough to have it stuck on all her tin boxes.

On the 26th day of their journey the little convoy finally arrived at the confluence of the Ganges and Jumna rivers and the site of the ancient Hindu city of Prayag,

renamed Allahabad by the Mughal emperor Akbar. At last, Char could write joyfully to the Queen to say that she found her husband well and in excellent spirits. It was a 'great happiness to be with him again after an absence of 7 months!' and Minny Stuart was able to report how cheering it was to see 'the bright look in Char's eyes, as she came in to dinner with her light step'. Only young Stanley was not impressed. 'Here I am & as odious a place as can be imagined', was how he began his first, brief letter from Allahabad:

> I saw Lord Canning in the evening he is not much changed but his mouth is gone in more as he never wears his false teeth now. Ldy C is very happy now she has come back to him. Bouverie [ADC] goes down in 4 days in charge of the King of Oudh's Jewels, 600,000 £ worth, & Bowie with him so Baring & I are left to do the whole duty, now Lady Canning will exhaust an ordinarily strong person to herself alone now goodbye

Allahabad had not yet recovered from the previous year's devastation. Char found it to be a place 'where people live almost as in a camp' and the 'small rather shabby house' occupied by her husband one of the very few European bungalows that had not been burned to the ground. She filled it with furniture brought up

Country boats moored at evening time near Bhaugulpore (Bhagalpur), August 1858. 'The actual journey is not so pleasant as I expected', wrote Char to her mother at this stage of her journey. 'I never can describe the horror of the live nature moving about the cabin & the dinner-table, especially one pale insect as big as a bird! which might give one a nightmare. It is preserved in spirits, & I shall hope one day to show it to you, & you will feel for me when you know that it was – on my throat!'

in the barge and was soon renewing old acquaintances over the dinner table. She was particularly pleased to see more of Sir Colin Campbell, soon to be ennobled as Lord Clyde – a 'nasty smelling ugly man he is', thought Johnny Stanley. However, the unusually fierce heat, made worse by the delayed arrival of the rains, only intensified Char's preoccupation with her husband's health. 'He looks well but is much worn', was an often repeated refrain in her letters, usually coupled with the hope that Charles might find some respite from the heat: 'The thing I have at heart is that he shall take measures to keep away from Calcutta in the next hot season and rains.'

This excessive concern would seem to have contributed to the unhappy circumstances that young Johnny Stanley observed and reported with his customary candour in his second letter from Allahabad, written a mere six weeks after their arrival:

> My dear Mamma,
> (This is private) I do not like the way the G.G. treats Lady Canning, she is constantly thinking only of him & how to please him & he is as sulky as possible & last night at dinner he snubbed her dreadfully for nothing & her poor face looked so pained, she tried to laugh it off but it was a very agonised laugh. I wd go a good way to save her such a scene as that for she is as proud as possibly can be with all her devotion to him.

Absence, it seems, had not made Lord Canning's heart grow fonder. It appears that their marriage was no happier now than it had been prior to their departure for India, although Johnny Stanley did add a brief postscript to this comment of his some nine months later that showed the Governor-General in a rather better light. 'I think I wrote something about Lord & Lady Canning implying they were not quite as happy as one might expect', he stated. 'Still I see that he is jealously alive to any slight that might be put upon her.'

Whatever strains there may have been in their relationship, Charlotte Canning was far too proud and self-disciplined to betray signs of weakness, to the extent that to casual observers she sometimes appeared to be quite as aloof as her husband. Yet Johnny Stanley found this hard to believe: 'I have been told by several persons, when I remarked how very popular Lady Canning must be that I have only seen her bright side & that last year she used to be very cold & proud. I said to myself, no wonder with such snobs as she has to talk to.'

Johnny had been horrified on his arrival at Allahabad to find the Governor-General even more overburdened than before: 'Ld C's arrears of work are sometimes tremendous, his room is full of boxes not opened even.' As well as overseeing the restoration of order in the country Lord Canning was now deep in the throes of augmenting a major constitutional change. The old system of government by a trading company on behalf of Britain was to be replaced by British Crown rule, with Lord Canning as the Queen's first Viceroy. It was not a change that John Stanley approved of. 'I like John Company [the East India Company] & don't see why he has to be turned out', he grumbled. 'No one thinks the Queen's Government will manage better.' This major transformation was heralded by the appearance in the autumn skies of a great comet, 'so clear & pale in colour and with such a magnificent tail, the nucleus as bright as a moon'. When large numbers of frogs began congregating in his room, Johnny concluded that it was the comet's doing: 'The natives all say it shows a change of dynasty so they are told it heralds the Queen's Govt coming in.' Char had heard the same story. 'All change is attributed to the comet. It frightens the natives but they said it was a good omen for [the] English – The King of Delhi must have left Delhi when it was high in the sky & the omen of the end of his dynasty is very much to the point.'

Crown rule comes to India: the royal proclamation read from the steps of Government House, Calcutta, on 1 November 1858. The curious tracery covering the building is bamboo scaffolding, which was erected to support the evening's illuminations.

The transfer of government was to be announced in the form of a royal proclamation – parts of it written by Queen Victoria herself – which was to be promulgated simultaneously at Allahabad and up and down the country on 1 November 1858, a day that Char found to be particularly auspicious. 'I do not know if any one but myself was struck with the coincidence of having accidentally chosen All Saints Day for this ceremony', she wrote to the Queen on the day after the proclamation. 'When I was reading over the epistle for the day by myself it felt a strangely striking coincidence to read of the pardon & merciful message to the great multitude, many nations & tongues! May it not be an omen for good?' Despite the local populace's cautious response, Char thought the proceedings had gone off very well:

> Lord Canning with Ld Clyde & Sir W Mansfield and their respective staffs assembled in the Fort and rode out with the Body Guard to an open Semiana [Shamiana] or raised tent of scarlet cloth with the Royal arms and flags on the Glacis overlooking the plain. The natives stood below & the official people & their subordinates were in raised seats & the troops drawn up all round. The natives had some misunderstanding of the subject & not much more than 2000 were present. Lord Canning gave the Proclamation to the Chief Secretary, Mr Edmonstone, who read it aloud in English and Urdu and said it exceedingly well & I believe delighted the natives who were near enough to hear. The evening ended with fireworks which is the display which most delights natives. Tonight they illuminate their own houses and have anxiously expressed a wish that he should drive through the streets to see it. There has hardly been time yet to hear much of the effect of the Proclamation upon them.

Late that same evening Johnny Stanley sat down to give his impressions of the Viceroy's tour through the streets: 'My dear Mamma,' he began. 'We have just got back from a drive through the town, Ld. C. for the first time in India was cheered, he was quite touched & so confused & agitated he made a very stupid remark to me which I very kindly would not notice.' Johnny himself was still much preoccupied with his feuding:

> I will give you an example of Mrs. Stuart's meddling & mischief making. I went yesterday to see the King of Delhi, the man who has the care of him had, it seems, orders to let no one in, however he made no difficulty with me, & I saw him, the miserable old man, I must say it shocked me very much, in a wretched tent on a common bed. He lay half sitting up trying to smoke his long pipe, his pyjamas were most common & he looked most unregal. I must say I was told I must not show him any respect & so went in with my cap on – I could not help as I left him touching my cap, for willingly as I might help to harry him he is too decrepit & old & one can feel nothing but pity for him. Well, having told Lady C. about

> it, I tell her everything, Mrs. S. was by & heard & afterwards at dinner told Lord C., he was very angry as orders had been given that no one was to be allowed to see the King, & I was the cause of the poor man getting into a scrape. All yesterday a fierce correspondence went on between me & Mrs. S.

The unfortunate Mrs S. was the butt of another Stanley jibe a few weeks later when she made what was evidently a malapropism. 'Fancy Mrs Stuart told me yesterday I was flatulent – Lady C. & I had to hide our faces', wrote the delighted Johnny.

Christmas came and went in Allahabad without major incident. 'The last few weeks since the great day of the Proclamation have not been very eventful', wrote Charlotte to the Queen. Lord Clyde was pursuing the last remaining body of enemy troops and Char thought it noteworthy that local people no longer offered them any support: 'The Magistrates of a part of the country they passed thru' found the people again tilling their fields as if nothing had happened. He questioned them & found them [the rebels] spoken of in such terms of abuse that the Secretary was shy about giving the translation! This certainly looks as if they strongly felt that the fugitives were on the losing side.' Char was also able to report that a number of locally recruited European nurses had begun working in the military hospitals: 'It has been a great comfort to the men & this trial has worked exceedingly well.' Even so, she was against more nurses being brought out from England. These now employed knew India and its ways and were 'in that respect more useful than any we could get from England'.

A month later Char was informing the Queen of her imminent departure for Calcutta, this time by road:

> I am in a few minutes to begin my journey there. It is not a pleasant prospect, for tho' the road is excellent travelling is in a rude state & my party fills 8 carriages drawn each by one pony & conveying by night only one person inside. Lord Canning remains here 4 days more for his party fills 11 carriages & we take up the whole fast dak [stage] traffic of the road & cannot go together – I think of being quite alone in the long nights, & drawn by wicked horses any thing but pleasant.

Minny Stuart was included in the advance party – but not Johnny Stanley. 'Little Johnny was left behind with Lord Canning,' noted Mrs Stuart with satisfaction, 'but cantered on his arab at the portière of his liege lady as far as he could.'

The much dreaded move down to Calcutta proved to be hard-going but without mishap. 'We only stopped twice a day to dress & eat and to change the carriage into the shape of a bed at night', wrote Char on 9 February to the Queen. 'The miserable unbroken horses somehow always did their work galloping the 5 mile stage without stopping when once pushed off and the fight & resistance they invariably make, overcome by force – I believe the speculators deliberately work them to death rather than find good horses.'

In February 1859 the brief Cold Weather season in Bengal came to its usual abrupt end and soon Char was writing to her friend Lady Sydney to say that three years had passed and she could now 'dare to look forward to getting back again as the pleasantest thing in the world'. More than half the usual five-year term of office for a Governor-General was over.

Char had hoped to persuade her husband to spend their fourth Hot Weather in the hills but this time it was the reorganisation of India's finances that kept the Viceroy at Government House. Rather than be separated from him again Char preferred to stay and face the heat and humidity of Bengal. 'I do not know how Lady Canning can stand it', wrote Johnny Stanley to his parents. 'She always says, "Oh I can do anything", but she is not looking well at all.' However, it was Minny Stuart who was the worst casualty of the heat. She became increasingly unwell and was advised by Dr Leckie to return immediately to England. This she refused to do – 'unless I saw a prospect of any one being able to come to Char to take my place'. It was eventually agreed that the Stuarts should leave in July, the role of Military Secretary being taken over by Major Sir Edward Campbell, Bt, who two years earlier had distinguished himself on Delhi Ridge with the 60th Rifles. However, with two small children to look after, Lady Campbell was to be no substitute for Minny Stuart.

Indeed, Lady Canning's close court circle was now fast breaking up. Dr Leckie, for so long her main informant on Indian matters and Anglo-Indian customs, was being replaced by a younger man, Dr Beale, while the stalwart Major Bowie went off on Home leave in March. Perhaps the sorriest to see the latter go was Johnny Stanley, even though he made Major Bowie 'nearly faint by telling him he was going home in the same ship as Mrs Stuart'. Johnny himself, after more than a year under Charlotte Canning's wing, was beginning to show signs of improvement. 'I do not think he is quite as hostile to dark skins as he was', Char was able to write to Johnny's mother, adding that she was endeavouring to keep him in 'very good order'. Johnny, too, was eager to show his parents that he was a reformed character: 'Lady C. (quite private) has at last confessed that Mrs Stuart is wanting in tact & tiresome sometimes & she told me she thinks (public again) that I, if anything, am too much the other way. Is not that a new character for me!' When in May Char received the news that her sister Louisa's husband, Lord Waterford, had been killed in a hunting accident, it was to Johnny that she first turned:

> The very next day that the telegram about Lord Waterford came, Lady Canning sent for me & talked to me about how miserable Lady W must be, tho' Mrs Stuart who went bouncing in directly the news came naturally got a snub – she said afterwards to me 'Lady C. is very odd about her sorrows. She does not like showing any'. I said to myself 'How few could – to you'.

The Stuarts left Calcutta on 4 July, Colonel Stuart noting in his journal that after they had taken their leave of Charles Canning, Char had followed them to their room to say her goodbyes more privately. 'Poor thing!' He added. 'There is much to gratify her in her husband's grandeur of character and success, but her lines have not fallen in pleasant places here. God be with her!' To this was appended a further note written two and a half years later: 'I little thought that night that I was looking my last upon that most lovely, bright and intellectual countenance, sometimes radiant, more often sad; always one of the most expressive that ever was seen.'

With the Stuarts went a portfolio of Char's drawings, to be delivered to Lady Stuart de Rothesay in England. An earlier collection of her flower paintings, sent home the year before, had been admired by none other than the artist and critic John Ruskin. According to Lady Stuart de Rothesay, he had declared them to be 'the grandest representation of flowers he had ever seen', commenting particularly on the artist's 'subtle use of colour'.

For all Colonel Stuart's concern for his cousin, the months immediately following the Stuarts' departure were probably the happiest that both Char and Carlo Canning had known for many months. In August the Viceroy was persuaded to spend a week at Barrackpore, which was extended first by a fortnight and then by a further three weeks. Charles went in to Calcutta only once a week to attend the Council meetings and in between times actually allowed himself some time off from his duties. In the process a reconciliation of sorts took place between husband and wife. Char's letters to friends and relatives written over this period were charged with an unexpected note of happiness. 'We have been here nearly a month – delighted to be in the country. C. has liked it this time', she told Lady Sydney. 'Being here is the greatest treat for me', she informed her mother. 'I have enjoyed 5 weeks here very much indeed. C. drives about in a phaeton, and I have gone out to sketch morning & evening.' To the Queen she wrote of the 'endless pleasure' it gave her to be at Barrackpore, 'so enjoyable, so green, & the foliage so luxuriant'. This same letter, written on 22 August, also conveyed news of an ambitious camping tour being organised for the Viceroy, one that would take him hundreds of miles across Northern India. Its purpose was to underline the fact that the Pax Britannica had been restored:

OPPOSITE Charlotte Canning at work on one of her flower studies, *c.* 1860.

> I hope he will march over much of the country and judge of many matters with his own eyes, and give the loyally disposed an opportunity of tendering their allegiance to Your Majesty. It will be one of the most interesting tours ever made, and it is thought necessary to move with a camp on a very large scale for in this country it is very necessary to speak to the eye and from time to time to pass thro' the country, & on such occasions reductions are not true economy.
>
> The exact line of march will be settled in a few weeks, when the different residents have reported on the state of the country around them and it can be decided where their final acts of pacification will be most effectual. We shall certainly go thro' Oude & to Agra & Delhi, perhaps into Bundelkund & eventually to Simla & very far north.

Two months later Char, along with her two maids, was installed in her own suite of tents at the centre of a vast encampment outside the ruins of Cawnpore – and grumbling a little into a special journal of the tour which she was writing up for her mother and sister that she could not 'quite go into ecstasies about camp-life'.

The Viceroy's Camp in a mango grove at La Martiniere, on the outskirts of Lucknow, 28 October 1859. The Cannings remained here during their visit to the city.

In a long letter written on 2 November she gave the Queen a full account of her experiences:

Madam,
I think your Majesty will like to hear from me after my first experience of camp life and one visit to Oude and the sight of so many places in which Your Majesty has felt such deep interest. I joined Lord Canning here 2 days after his arrival in camp about a fortnight ago, and we yesterday returned from Oude having spent a week in Lucknow.

Ld Clyde was here and marched with his camp at the same time and the entry into the town [Lucknow] was made with very great state, with all the Escort and all the Garrison. Ld Canning & Ld Clyde rode & I followed them in the carriage, and our procession of nearly two miles in length wound along the new roads thro' the town and past all the spots of which we have heard & thought so much until we reached our camp under the shade of the great mango trees of the Martiniere.

I wish your Majesty could see your troops on this sort of occasion – Artillery, Bays, the remains of the Light Cavalry, 2 Irregular regiments of Seiks & Punjabees in their wild native dress, one earth coloured, the other blue, & then the 2nd Battn Rifle Brigade, the 35th & 73rd, a sepoy regiment of rearmed well behaved remnants, 2 Seik regts, some Bengal artillery & then the Heavy Guns – 2 of them 24 lb. drawn each by 11 pair of milk white bullocks, the drivers sitting on the yoke & dressed in white with red turbans.

The Talookdars who were all summoned to the Great Durbar were ranged in a new great square near the Kaiser Bagh, standing by the side of their horses & I believe they were allowed to remount & join in the Procession. I hear they went away from Lucknow in a much happier state of mind than they came to it for every mysterious terror had taken hold of them & their relatives in some cases came to weep over them as doomed men! As it is they go back in possession of their lands, and with a very different account of their reception from their anticipation. 180 Talookdars were summoned. About 20 less than that number came, but of these most had real reasons of absence such as sickness – a few kept away from fear but many frightened men came and one owned that his neighbour said to him 'now our time is come' when the guard of honour & the guns prepared for the salute.

Ld Canning received the 9 who had saved British lives separately & they afterwards at the Durbar received their presents & rewards. It was most interesting to hear & see (I did both through a small peeping place where my presence could not be perceived). It was a beautiful sight. I believe by far the largest Durbar there has ever been. The great tent had full 500 people in it. The chiefs are not very handsome & I believe they keep to the old habit of thinking it prudent to try & look poor when near to those who they think might lay hold of their riches in any shape.

> It is not usual to make any kind of speech at a Durbar, but on this occasion Ld Canning felt it wd be of use and I think Your Majesty will read & approve of his speech. It has had an undoubtedly good effect and there is good hope of these wild men turning into loyal subjects.

Between their official engagements the Cannings toured the scenes of nine months of continuous fighting:

> Lucknow is very well worth seeing even now – but one can hardly imagine anything more picturesque than its old state. Many of the gilt domes are destroyed but enough remain to be gay & peculiar, and some of the buildings about the Imambara now enclosed in the Fort are most striking – It must be owned that all is plasterwork. We were shown every spot by officers who stood the siege & it was like a dream to feel oneself really there after the intense anxiety one had felt for that devoted Garrison! The houses have many of them disappeared but 8 or 9 still stand and are really as covered with shot marks as an old Target wd be, & inside & out you see traces of round shot & shells. One very interesting thing was to ride over the actual line of march of the relief & the withdrawal of the Garrison. We made Lord Clyde take us along every step of the way & he told many anecdotes at every point. Two early mornings were spent in this. The points of dense fighting along this line and Havelock's advance are still riddled with shot.

Returning from Lucknow to Cawnpore, Char had to brace herself for a visit to the sites of the two massacres:

> I am tomorrow to go over the sad scenes here with Captain Mowbray Thomson, one of the 4 survivors of the massacre. I own I pity him very much for finding his appointment in the Police has brought him back to this spot. I suppose it is one's impression of the horrors which have happened here which throw such a gloom over the place, but I think I never saw anything so hopelessly arid and gloomy. Ruined houses everywhere and every spot with a story of horror. We are to choose the site of the memorial church tomorrow & to lay out the ground round the well. The design of the memorial monument will be chosen from some expected from England.

In the event, it was Char's own design for a statue of the Angel of the Resurrection – 'the only thought which can calm sorrow or bring comfort in connection with the awful catastrophe' – that, with only slight modifications, became the model

OPPOSITE Preparing for the Durbar at Fatehgur, 15 November 1859.
BELOW The holy tank of Manasi Ganga at Gobardan near Muttra, a centre of pilgrimage for Hindus. December 1859.

for Baron Marochetti's marble statue. Her letter ended with a detailed account of the rigours of life under canvas:

> We stay two days more for the Bundelkund chiefs have come across from Calpee for a great Durbar & the Rajah of Rewah & the Benares Rajah. From thence we march to Futteyghur & Agra.
>
> The march from ten to 12 or 13 miles is performed in early morning & the sight is very curious – such a stream of men & beasts, camels & elephants. We have a large escort, the 35th., 2 squadrons of the Bays, a battery of horse artillery, an irregular Seik [Sikh] cavalry regiment & a Sikh infantry & the Body Guard. I believe these troops are being naturally moved in this direction & will be changed when convenient. One gets to know many of the faces passing them each day in the line of march. As yet we have kept to our own carriage & horses but I believe it is usual to ride where one can go across country & keep out of the clouds of dust. The double set of tents goes on overnight and we find in each place our own street in the midst of a sea of tents. It is curious to see how common domestic arrangements go on in India apparently without the slightest effort, and at each station the tents grow & the tables are spread & fifty or more people are asked to dine & entertained just as they might be at Calcutta.
>
> I own I do not in all things think the life in camp one of complete delight as is generally represented: getting up every day in the dark, & going thru' the extremes of cold & heat is hardly pleasant – 50° & 95° in a tent the same day – I never knew what heat was till I came here & the damp moist air of Calcutta is to me far less trying than this parching climate, but I am told it is to be quite different soon – the dust alone excepted, which is perpetual.

As her Viceroy began to lead his great caravan northwards towards Agra, the monarch in whose name he journeyed set down her own thoughts on this grand imperial progress:

> To see India & above all to <u>show</u> personally my <u>great anxiety</u> for the welfare of my Indian <u>subjects</u>, would be a <u>great</u> pleasure for me for I <u>do</u> feel so anxious that <u>kindness</u> & a <u>deep</u> regard for their feelings & susceptibilities, & strict & impartial justice, coupled with requisite firmness should not only usher in the <u>commencement</u> of a <u>new order</u> of things but that the Indians should be accustomed to <u>look</u> upon <u>these</u> as principles of their Queen and her Government!

OPPOSITE The Viceroy's party leaves Agra Fort to inspect the Taj Mahal, November 1859.
BELOW The Viceroy and escort return from Fort Jamrud after inspecting the nearby Khyber Pass, February 1860.

OVERLEAF The memorial well and church built at Cawnpore to commemorate the two massacres of 1857. Baron Marochetti's Angel of the Resurrection, placed over the well itself, followed Charlotte Canning's design in virtually every respect other than having two palm fronds rather than one.

THE MEMORIAL CHURCH

MAROCHETTI'S MONUMENT OVER THE WELL

MEMORIAL BUILDING AND GARDENS

CHAPTER IX

'A Wild Journey'

The progress of the Viceroy's 'Camp' across the Northern Indian plains was like the advance of an army. For Lord and Lady Canning, their staff and entourage alone, 150 large tents were pitched along the main street of the camp, requiring 80 elephants and 500 camels for their transport. Another 500 camels, 500 bullocks and 100 bullock carts were used for transporting their equipage, 527 coolies to carry the glass windows belonging to the larger tents, 100 *bhistis* or water carriers to water the camp streets and keep down the dust and 40 sweepers to keep them clean. In addition, there were 40 riding elephants, innumerable private baggage animals and horses for riding and driving, together with all their keepers and grooms and a multitude of attendant camp followers – totalling in all not less than 20,000 men, women and children. On the line of march they spread out along 24 miles of road, the advance guard arriving at the ground to be occupied on the following day as the rear guard pulled out of the camp site occupied the night before.

The job of keeping this vast caravan on the road had been given to a young officer named Fred Roberts, who had fought with great distinction through virtually every Mutiny campaign and was to rise to the very top of his profession as Field Marshal Lord Roberts. It was he who had led the Viceroy's parade through Lucknow, observing what Lady Canning's sense of delicacy had evidently prevented her from mentioning in her letter to the Queen: that the streets were lined with hostile Indians 'who – cowed, but not tamed – looked on in sullen defiance, very few showing any sign of respect for the Viceroy'.

In his autobiography, *Forty-One Years in India*, Lord Roberts recalled with great warmth his first meeting with the 'gentle, gracious lady, whose unaffected and simple, yet perfectly dignified manner' made such a deep impression that both he and his wife, 'in common with everyone who was at all intimately associated with Lady Canning', became devoted to her. Even while on the line of march the Cannings entertained large parties to dinner on most nights and the Roberts marvelled at the effort Charlotte Canning put into making these rather stuffy occasions more enjoyable: 'The shyest person was set at ease by her kindly, sympathetic

The 'main street' of the Viceroy's Camp. Lady Canning's tents were always pitched on the left side of the central dining-tent, Lord Canning's on the right.

manner, and she had the happy knack of making her guests feel that her entertainments were a pleasure to herself – the surest way of rendering them enjoyable to those she entertained.' In camp just as in Calcutta Char assiduously set about making friends, building up a huge circle of acquaintances from among the civil and military castes of British India. Though she found this entertaining 'the most fatiguing part of this camp-travelling, for at every large place we have the whole community to dinner, up to 50, 60, or even 69 every day', it amused her to think of the numbers of people she was getting to know: 'I always knew a great many people, and what it will be after making acquaintance with three-fourths of the army list and the whole civil service of India, is alarming to think of.' Quietly and perhaps even unconsciously, Char was performing a most valuable service to her husband's office, for if few got to know her intimately a great many came to look upon her with real affection and admiration. A Viceroy could hardly have asked more of his Vicereine.

After the second viceregal durbar at Cawnpore on 2 November – significant for Canning's declaration to the Indian Princes acknowledging their right to adopt heirs – the camp moved up to Fatehgarh for a third durbar on the 15th. Then it went westwards for nine marches to Agra, the old Mughal capital in the sixteenth and seventeenth centuries, guarded by the massive red sandstone fort that looks out across a bend of the Jumna River at the Taj Mahal.

Char was expecting to be thoroughly let down by the Taj. 'It is no exaggeration to say that I have had it detailed to me many hundred times in the last four years', she told the Queen – yet she found it 'impossible to be disappointed. I believe I have seen all the great works of the moors in Europe & none approach this.

The whole is so pure in its white marble & pietra dura tracery and from its dome to its base all so gigantic & of such delicate finish.' During her twelve days at Agra she found 'a wealth of subjects for her facile pen', returning time and again to the Taj gardens to sketch and paint from different points of view and under different conditions of light – even making the traditional moonlight pilgrimage.

At dawn on 9 December the viceregal tents were struck once more and the caravan moved towards Meerut. Three nights later disaster struck. 'It was all done by a new stove, lit for the first time', Char wrote later to her mother. 'I opened my eyes at 12½ o'clock to the bright light of the flame. It was a great mercy I saw it so instantly, for half a minute later would have been a frightful sight. I had slept, but I think I was awake or I should have felt more startled, and it was very little when I first saw it coming out of the inner partition of my tent.' With great presence of mind Char ran out and ordered the British sentry outside to sound the alarm. She then ran round the large dinner tent that separated her own quarters from her husband's and forced her way past an Indian sentry to wake him: 'So little did I think the fire was upon us, that I could tell him to put on some clothes, and the fire never did get to that tent, for they struck it out in time, and only his writing tent was burnt, and two passages besides my poor tent. He lost very few papers, but all his furniture, and some old boxes. The maids' tent was not burnt, but they woke at the sight of the flames of mine and fled in their quilts. They behaved quite well.'

Running back to her own tent, Char tried to save some of her own belongings. However, the roof was now well ablaze and despite Char's brave efforts she was

Sowars (troopers) of the escorting Punjab Horse and sepoys of the Viceroy's Bodyguard in camp.

able to save very little: 'I knew I was quite safe & unhurt, and could run in and out of the burning tent, and I knew nobody else was in the tent, so, except for sorrow for my goods and the tent, and a great wish to see the other tents divided off, I had nothing to dread.' Her first thought was for her drawings and journals:

> I thought I had saved them so cleverly, dragging the bundle of portfolios quite clear of the tent, and it was the only thing I saved. But I believe an outer awning fell on them afterwards, for certainly they were burnt, though every one who could pick them up did so. All my journals were burnt an inch round, and the last entirely. All drawings were burnt round, and much scattered and trodden down. I had nothing left from the fire but my night-gown, dressing-gown, one boot and one stocking, and a hat in the maid's tent. Lord Clyde brought me an enormous dressing-gown and everybody contributed something.

It was equally characteristic of Charlotte Canning that the last thing she should think of saving were in conventional terms the most valuable:

> My jewels had the narrowest escape. I did not think of them till about 10 minutes after the fire began, when I was reflecting over the contents of my tent, and every one was at the burning mass. Then an officer I hardly knew came by, and I sent him off to pull my two imperials out of the fire. I believe the man was so taken aback by the sight of me in my blue flannel, with streaming hair, standing alone in the moonlight in the middle of the camp, that he could not listen to the accurate direction I gave of the position of the boxes. Presently I saw Sir E. Campbell, who went off like a shot after them, had water thrown over the boxes and rummaged them instantly, and brought out my pearls, all but on fire, but still safe. All my other jewels were more or less black, but many safe.

The fire was prevented from spreading any further by the Sikhs on guard duty who cut down the guy-ropes of the nearby tents with their *talwars*. When Fred Roberts, who was with the advance camp, saw the Cannings next morning, Charlotte was wearing Lady Campbell's clothes – 'and as Lady Canning was tall, and Lady Campbell was short, the effect was rather funny'. Fortunately, Char had sent part of her wardrobe on ahead and was soon able to return what she had borrowed. Never one to dwell on her own misfortunes, Char made light of her loss when she next wrote to Queen Victoria – only expressing polite distress that her portrait of the Queen had been 'a good deal scorched & discoloured & I fear will never recover'. This was something that could – and was – easily made good, but the destruction of so many of Char's paintings, letters and journals was a real blow. 'When I remember how you toiled, weary, tired, and hating it', wrote her old friend Minny Stuart, after hearing of the fire, 'to keep that record of an unprecedented trial and era, it seems as if I would have sacrificed even your pearls to have kept those books.'

The New Year was seen in somewhere on the plains between Meerut and Delhi. 'Another new year since last I wrote', Char was able to state with some satisfaction in a letter to her mother. 'How I like to think we can now say "next year" for getting back to you all.' After three months under canvas she was beginning to find that this outdoor life improved 'with habit' and had its advantages: 'I must say this camp life, and seeing so many new people, and hearing of so much settled, looks as if it got through more work than months of writing and piles of red boxes at Calcutta.' The weather had become almost English in its mildness and no longer shifted so violently in its daily range of temperatures, allowing her to 'go out and sketch every afternoon on an elephant'.

From Delhi – which was 'not to be compared to Agra. All is in such decadence

Livestock grazing under the walls of Sirhind in the Punjab, a fort destroyed by the Sikhs in 1763. 25 January 1860.

one can hardly judge what it was' – the viceregal camp progressed northwards to Umballa (Ambala, today) and on 29 January crossed the Sutlej, the first of the five rivers of the Punjab. As the Sikh rulers of the Punjab princely states came in turn to receive rewards for their loyal support of the British during the 1857–8 uprising, there were more 'brilliant shows' to be witnessed, culminating in a 'dazzling cavalcade' of caparisoned elephants, horses and marching troops as Lord Canning made his state entry into Lahore – a day of magnificent spectacle marred only by a stampede of the riding elephants during the evening's firework display, which provoked a badly shaken Lord Clyde to declare that a general action was

OPPOSITE The Taj Mahal: one of a number of views painted by Charlotte Canning over several days in November 1859.
BELOW A 'dazzling cavalcade': the triumphant entry into Lahore – marred by the rout of the elephants. A watercolour by Sir Edward Campbell, himself a talented amateur artist.

Govindgarh, the fort at Amritsar, built by Sikh Emperor Ranjit Singh. February 1860.

Water pavilions of the palace at Deeg, built by the Jat war-lord Raja Sural Mal of Bharatpur in the early eighteenth century.

The famous Shalimar Gardens outside Lahore with their three hundred fountains, laid out by the Mughal Emperor Shah Jehan.

not half so dangerous. Here Lord Canning held the last and most colourful of his formal durbars.

After a week in Lahore the Viceroy's camp was split up. The main body was sent off north-east to Sialkot while a much smaller contingent headed by the Viceroy paid a flying visit to Peshawar and the extreme north-western corner of the subcontinent. Lord Canning was anxious to determine by personal observation whether the frontier boundary should be maintained where it was or pulled back to the Indus River. Since Charlotte Canning was equally determined to see this remote corner of British India she followed in her own party a day later, travelling in a carriage drawn by relays of camels. 'It was a great fatigue,' she admitted to her mother, 'but I am glad to have seen this strange country and the actual boundary of India, and the very door of it, which is really the case at the entrance of the Khyber Pass.' The Cannings inspected this most notorious of defiles at a

OPPOSITE The main street and temple of Kangra, set against the Himalayan snows, March 1860.

respectful distance – 'for people run the risk of a shot if they go very near' – before the Viceroy pronounced himself satisfied that that 'natural wall of mountain with its few passes' made a far better frontier than a river. The local Afghans struck Char as being 'the finest race of people I have ever seen, and convince me easily as to their being the remnant of the lost tribes'.

The return journey from Peshawar to Sialkot was marred by what could have been a very serious accident when Lady Canning's maid, Rain, 'nearly managed to kill herself, by taking fright at the camels running away, and jumping out of the carriage. She fell on the back of her head and bruised her back, but is doing quite well.' This was just as well because Rain had become engaged to a Mr Fitz-Squires during the long march and the couple had made arrangements to get married at Simla. Her employer was not as keen on the idea as she might have been: 'I shall mind it dreadfully for my personal comfort, as she has been an admirable and sensible maid for 11 or 12 years.'

Before Simla – and the end of almost six months' march over more than a thousand miles – the beginnings of another Hot Weather had to be endured. 'The heat of the last week in tents for many hours of each day was quite unbearable', Char told the Queen; 'Lord Canning felt it exceedingly & was quite knocked up by it. At the last encampment near the hills we gladly took refuge in some beautiful gardens & summer houses of the Pathiala Raja where fountains played & running water & shade.' Another more ambitious diversion during this return march took the Cannings up the Beas valley to Kangra and Dharamsala, two

The camel cart in which Lady Canning travelled post-haste from Lahore to Peshawar.

Maharaja Ranjit Singh of Kashmir offering gifts to the Viceroy, Lord Canning, at Durbar in Sialkot, 9 March 1860. An engraving from a drawing by the professional artist William Simpson, who accompanied the Viceroy on his tour.

The ancient bastion of Attock, guarding the crossing of the Indus. February 1860.

mountain villages set deep in the foothills of the Himalayas, where Charles Canning was able to have his first taste of crisp cold air for four years. However, even this short escape from the heat was not to be compared to what was being planned as the Viceroy's first summer in the hills, to be spent in Simla, the British hill station perched eight thousand feet above the plains.

Waiting for Lady Canning at Barnes Court, one of Simla's typically Gothic-style half-timbered summer residences, was a slightly tetchy letter from the Queen complaining that Char's letters were becoming less frequent: 'It is more than 2 months since I had a letter, and your letters are always so welcome. I was in hopes of hearing from you but will not delay writing longer. I send you the long promised set of photographs of the whole family.' In fact, three months had passed since Char had last written, shortly after the fire in camp, and she hastened to thank the Queen for the photographs, commenting that 'the growth of the younger Princesses is very apparent but I do not feel puzzled in tracing their likeness, dated in my recollections of four & a half years ago when they were quite little children'. The account she gave of their travels through the Punjab and up to Peshawar were no more than cursory, however, for Char was preoccupied with events closer at hand. Her eagerly anticipated holiday with her husband had been cut short and Lord Canning was hurrying back to Calcutta:

> I have been bitterly disappointed to find that Ld Canning must at once leave & return to Calcutta. He had promised Sir J. Outram to relieve him of his duties as President of the Council if he fell ill and wished to leave it, & a telegram has arrived saying he must leave off work or his life will be condemned. Ld Canning will travel towards Calcutta on May 7, the hottest part of the year. He has himself been suffering from a violent attack of brow ague, but has just now recovered & I had hoped he would work with additional vigour & comfort to himself at the same time as he enjoyed this delightful climate & its strangely grand scenery.

Writing to her mother, Char was more outspoken in her language: 'It is so very provoking that I can hardly bear to think of it: he will not hear of my going.' And if her view of this most spectacular of hill resorts appeared a little jaundiced it was perfectly understandable:

> I think the beauty of this place very questionable, it is such a sea of hill-tops, and the snowy mountains are so far off, and the dryness makes all look wintry.

OPPOSITE ABOVE Crossing a bridge of boats over the Beas river, in the heart of the Punjab, 3 February 1860.

BELOW The picturesque ruins of Rohtas, extending over 260 acres beside the Jhelum River, Punjab.

> But the deodar woods are fine: they are like cedar when old, and larch when young. There is ilex of a peculiar sort, and pinus longifolia like large pineasters, and very fine rhododendrons, but they are nearly over, and there is nothing else. The small shrubs are berberries and St John's wort: all besides is dried up. Some views are fine, but there are no straight lines, and not a spot of level ground. Here if one sees ten yards level, one screams out, 'What a site for a house!' Your chintzes and white papers have made this house look very nice; but alas! we shall have little use for it, though I suppose Lady Campbell and I must stay here till June or nearly July.

However, in an effort to cheer up Lady Canning an imaginative proposal was being considered which, when put to her a week later, won her immediate and enthusiastic acceptance. Now her tone was very different:

> A very tempting and enterprising plan has been made for me of reaching Mussouri by a long circuit round by 'Chini' on the borders of Thibet, over a pass, and in all ways tempting. C. at once liked the notion of sending me on such a lark, and I have quite entered into it, and shall go, for I am not fond of this place, and should, of course, avoid all society. I shall have no riding, but be carried in sort of chairs all the journey, and shall have bungalows to sleep in for a week, and tents afterwards. C. envies me, but could never have gone so much out of the way of telegraphs. I should have liked going too with C. to Calcutta far the best of all, and would not in the least have feared the heat, but C. would not for an instant hear of it, and I think he puts me very much off his conscience now this pleasant expedition in mountain air is planned.

Charles Canning, of course, had no more idea of what he was letting his wife in for than she did. Mussoorie was a more humble version of Simla, barely seventy miles off as the crow flies. But the route being proposed would take her right through the central Himalayan range along a deep cleft cut by the waters of the Sutlej, then up a side valley, back over the main range itself and down into the headwaters of the Jumna. It was very far from being the gentle ramble over hill and dale then considered fit for ladies seeking outdoor exercise and excitement. Indeed, when it was over Char herself did 'rather wonder at people recommending me this tour, for I certainly could hardly have called the roads passable, and I should scarcely advise any of my female acquaintances to go'.

When the Viceroy left he took with him his Military Secretary, Sir Edward Campbell, his Political Secretary, Mr Bowring, and Dr Beale, together with

OPPOSITE A giant deodar on the Nachar road, near Simla. This was one of two paintings of deodar cedars by Charlotte Canning reproduced by Edward Ravenscroft in his three-volume *Pinetum Britannicum*, which appeared in 1864.

Johnny Stanley – no doubt mortified at being excluded from Lady Canning's mountaineering expedition – and one other ADC. That left Captain Baring and Major Jones – 'who feels the heat dreadfully' – to look after the Vicereine. The local Commissioner, Lord William Hay, was also to accompany them. Lady Campbell – in Char's estimation the 'most gentle person I ever saw' and by now a close friend – was to stay behind in Simla with her two small children. 'It felt very much on my conscience to leave her alone,' wrote the kindhearted Char, 'but the children could not have come.' The lack of close companionship was the one disagreeable aspect of the trip. 'We shall be by no means lively', she confided to her old friend, Emily Lady Sydney. 'My three young gentlemen are of the very quietest description. You will think my scheme of travel a very wild one, but I believe I shall delight in it, and only want a comfortable and genial and strong female companion.' Of Simla she now had nothing kind to say: 'I have nothing whatever to tell you from these hill-tops. The place swarms with people, but I rather keep to out-of-the-way paths, and am alarmed at encountering the swarms of officers on leave, and smart ladies carried along in their "John Pons".' With her husband gone and the mountains beckoning the Simla 'Season' had no charms for her. One of her last engagements before she left was to attend Rain's wedding: 'She went off quite low at our parting, but our photographer happening to be at work and his plate ready, I did her spirits all the good in the world by making her "sit" in her wedding garments of white muslin, white silk bonnet, and a lace veil. She is a great loss to me, after nearly twelve years of excellent service. I do not think I ever once had to find a fault with her.' The very next morning Charlotte and her gentlemen companions were on their way, striking out northwards on horseback to join the Tibet trade route.

It was thirty-one days before the little expedition made its way up onto Mussoorie ridge. After a week's recuperation Char sat down to write the longest letter she had ever sent to the Queen, proud of what she had accomplished and in no mood to be humble about it, declaring that she sent 'this long story without apologies for I am sure no account of this portion of Your Majesty's dominions has ever been sent directly, or is ever likely to be sent, by one of Your Majesty's female subjects who has just visited it'. She began by explaining why she had undertaken this 'wild journey':

> When Lord Canning found his presence so necessary at Calcutta that he must travel down at the worst season of the year, I could not prevail upon him to let me go with him, & he insisted upon my remaining in the hills until the extreme

OPPOSITE Lady Canning with Lady Campbell under the deodars at Nachar, just outside Simla. Photographed by Sir Edward Campbell, April 1860.

heat had passed & the rains began to fall, & here I am still, awaiting the news of rain fallen in the plains.

Your Majesty will easily believe that I did not much like being left behind, so I think it was a good deal to comfort me that he strongly encouraged me to travel into the interior of the hills & see all I could of the highest mountains, all as far as Tibet. I consequently had a month's travelling & have been well repaid by all I have seen. I had the smallest possible camp & had with me two of Lord Canning's Aides de Camp, & Ld William Hay who is Commissioner of the Hill States, & my maid & servants. Everything had to be carried by coolies, & with every possible economy of baggage we made a long procession winding over the hill sides with all the stores & provisions & sheep & poultry & all the necessaries of life required in these wilds. For a week

Part of the 'Thibet Road' to Chini, photographed by Samuel Bourne three years after Lady Canning's adventurous journey.

I travelled along the Thibet road made by Ld Dalhousie. I went up the Sutledge valley as far as Chini, the place where Ld Dalhousie once went for three months to avoid the rains. No wonder they do not arrive there, for it is defended from them by a range of Peaks 21000 feet high. There is a moderate slope for a few miles about this place & it is rich with cultivation & Apricot trees & lower down with vineyards overhanging the Sutledge. The absence of Lakes and Glaciers makes this scenery far less beautiful than Switzerland, but I think the precipices & the enormous peaks are on a far grander scale. I am afraid that any sketches I can show will give no idea of these mountains & I so often was unable to attempt the finest scenes. Some walnut groves of gigantic trees & cedars with a background of pinnacles of rock & snow, being full 15,000 feet above, would have made a picture I shall always regret having failed to attempt.

I do not think settlers will ever be seen in any part of the country I have passed thru'. There never can be useful roads. The new [Dalhousie] road is in all the dangerous places impossible for two horsemen to meet in safety, at the best & widest it is but 6 ft. and after dwindles to 3. There is no level ground. The cultivation is in terraces on the smallest scale. The hill people seem happy & not poor. Their houses are substantial & of wood & stone like Swiss chalets & their clothes of blankets which they weave themselves in rude out of doors looms. I saw a great many of these people as so many were required to carry the tents & I thought them much more like Europeans than Indians. In the country near Chini many women carry the loads and I was prepared to feel distressed at the sight, but I found them so merry & chattering & so perfectly competent to scramble up the almost perpendicular roads without losing breath, that one's compassion vanished. They had a curious dress with enormous plaits of sheep's wool at the back of their heads, arranged like a caricature of the very fashionable young ladies au coiffées. Their blanket is draped like a statue & held together with an enormous brass brooch like the old Irish pattern.

All the country I passed thru' is under some Hill Rajah & I used always to be met by the chief people with gifts, of course accepting only some trifle such as a ball of musk or a yak's tail. The poor people of the village always brought milk & honey, or butter & walnuts. I saw very few of the Thibet people & regretted being unable to visit one of the Lama convents but I hardly liked to prolong my journey. Sometimes a Lama man or woman in her yellow dress appeared carrying a load with the other coolies. I saw Buddhism by the little temples with sort of urns painted, one white, one grey, & one yellow; or piles of engraved stones in the highways, always passed leaving them on the right hand. In one village I came upon large praying machines in wooden buildings like dog kennels. A prayer is written many times over inside & the roller revolves & is set spinning & praying by every passer by.

The letter also gave a long account of the many hazards encountered during their travels:

> To cross & recross the Sutledge I had to pass over the different sorts of bridges in use in these hills. The one kind made of trunks of trees reaching as far as possible, rising at an angle from the side & joined by two very long trees across the centre space; & to recross I was reminded of the Dee at Abergeldie for the Jhoola is on the same principle. It is however better in one respect for the passenger sits alone & is pulled across by ropes & suspended from 6 or 8 ropes over which a semicircle of wood runs from which the seat is fastened. I thought it decidedly less alarming than sitting in front of the Gardener on the 'cradle' of Abergeldie. I happily never came upon a third style of bridge over which the traveller has to walk on a rope. Between the Sutledge & the Jumna the mountains are very high & there are many passes. I came over the Roopin Pass which is considered the easiest. My camp was pitched at the edge of the snow in a dreary spot about 13000 feet high & next morning at peep of day we began to ascend. There were full 7 miles of snow to cross & we had dark glass 'goggles' & veils to protect the sight & gave all the scraps of muslins & veils that could be collected to the servants & coolies, but no one suffered. Sometimes the whole party is blinded by the glare & unable to see for a day or two & precautions are very necessary. The clouds did not allow a very complete view at the highest point but still most grand mountains came in sight. The highest part of the pass is 15480 feet. I had rather wished to go a little further up the sides to accomplish the exact height of Mt Blanc which could be easily done, but one has not breath for much activity at that height & I felt some compassion on my bearers who had carried me up so well. We used constantly to meet flocks of sheep & goats with little sacks laden with grain & goods of different kinds; a great number of these reached the summit of the Pass as we were sitting there busy in not very successful experiments of boiling water with a thermometer to see it boil at barely 180°, but our provision of spirits of wine fell short before the boiling point had been very distinctly reached.

At least part of the descent from the pass was 'rapid & delightful', with Charlotte Canning sliding down the snow slopes in what she referred to as a 'honey-pot' descent – 'not in the least improper, as I put on all my warmest clothing, & had an old Balmoral cloth riding-habit & a pair of strong dark cloth trousers'. Here her surroundings were most spectacular:

> The scenery in the descents with a river rushing out of snow caverns & frozen water falls & constant little avalanches was very striking. Then came the first vegetation sort of purple auriculas and other alpine plants & soon after rhododendrons, yellow instead of the pink sort of the Alps. My camp was that day well clear of the snow in birch woods with very fine purple Rhododendrons (the common scarlet kind grows much lower) and under enormous cliffs of rock just at the beginning of forests of fir. We had some disagreeable snow drifts to cross next day & used caution to avoid sliding down into snowy caverns & roaring streams under the snow. Most of the interest of the journey was over when we passed

out of the highest range & the last camps were cruelly hot, 97° in the tents. It was a sort of race against the rains which were liable to begin any day after the 20th so I was glad to reach this place by that day having made 27 marches – about 320 miles – & many of them very long ones & only four halts of a day each.

'Intensely interesting,' was Queen Victoria's comment on this remarkable adventure – 'but I think much of it sounded very dangerous.'

Three of Charlotte's drawings made during her month-long trek in the Himalayas in May-June 1860. All show a degree of artistic skill and confidence unmatched by her earlier work.
BELOW Porters and hill-men gathered beside a rest-house in a deodar grove at Taranda, in the Sutlej gorge.
OVERLEAF, LEFT Looking down from the 'Old Thibet Road' into a side valley joining the Sutlej at the Wangtu Bridge. RIGHT The village of Poaree perched above the Sutlej near Chini, the most northerly point of the journey.

CHAPTER X

'The Hard Trial of India'

The end of July 1860 found Charlotte Canning back in Government House, Calcutta, and in great spirit: '"It feels so like getting 'ome", as my maid West says, that I am very happy.' But delighted as Char was to be once more reunited with her husband she was a little put out to find him sporting a small goatee beard. 'Rather becoming in the abstract' though it might have been, its effect was to make Charles appear 'a different man, not the one I have been married to for nearly 25 years'.

The Rains that summer had been dangerously late in breaking, so much so that a disastrous drought and famine was being predicted. Up in Mussoorie Char had finally grown tired of waiting and had set off on another wild and uncomfortable dash in a closed coach across the plains, resting up during the day in dak bungalows and travelling by night. Whatever she had previously experienced by way of Hot Weather was as nothing compared to what she underwent on this five-day nightmare. 'I know now what heat is, which I really never knew before', she confessed. The hot winds of the plains were like 'the blasts of a furnace. The wind came in puffs, and felt as if it must leave scorch-marks upon one.' Char found that the only way to avoid this searing wind was to bury herself under a thick cloak. To her enormous relief the monsoon finally broke: 'I met the rain on the fifth night, and got well soaked in a thunderstorm, the carriage, I suppose, being open at every pore, and drinking in all it could.'

From Allahabad Lady Canning's party came down-river in comfort in the vice-regal flat, *Soonamookie*, as far as the newly-completed railhead at Rajmahal, where the ever-faithful Johnny Stanley was waiting for them. 'The train sent up to fetch us down from the Ganges was the first that had gone up to it', Char informed her mother. 'The railway people and engineers made a great event of this, and I hear it is called "tapping the Ganges". It cuts off a fine piece of way, and would

OPPOSITE Part of the vast encampment that accompanied Lord Canning's march across Northern India during the Cold Weather of 1859–60.

BELOW A cane bridge on the trail up to Darjeeling.

OVERLEAF Darjeeling: Buddhist prayer-flags and the Himalayan ranges to the north.

The last painting; an uncompleted watercolour of the edge of the terai jungle below Darjeeling. Here, according to Lady Bayley, 'She lingered on her journey returning to Calcutta in order to paint some flowers and orchids.' The word *terai* or 'moist land' was applied to the belt of jungle between the Ganges and the Himalayan foothills, notorious for its jungle fever.

have been an immense boon in 1857.' On a clear line with no stops the 205 miles from Rajmahal to Howrah Station in Calcutta were covered in eight hours – rather less time than the same journey takes today.

One of the Vicereine's first actions on returning was to despatch a parcel to the Queen containing some souvenirs of her travels:

> It contains some cloaks of Cashmeer embroidered at Delhi, and I shall be very happy if they are thought worthy of the acceptance of Your Majesty & the Princesses. The Black Cloak I had worked for Your Majesty, the white one for Princess Alice and the three smaller ones for the Princess Helena, Princess Louisa & Princess Beatrice. There are also some skins of different sorts of the Himalayan Pheasants which I hope will serve to make into trimmings for Riding hats. I could not have them cut and arranged here so I have ventured to send them in a rough state.

Char had assumed that her husband's term of office would come to an end before the start of the next Hot Weather, with Lord Elgin coming out as the next Viceroy. However, in mid-August the sudden death from dysentery of Lord Canning's chief financial adviser, James Wilson, who had been brought out at the Viceroy's request to rationalise the Indian Government's finances, put these hopes in jeopardy. When this was followed by the equally unexpected loss of the newly appointed Governor of Madras, Char's hopes were finally dashed. 'Pray do not leave off writing to us', she wrote in deep depression to Lady Sydney. 'Just now I want every consolation, for certainly next March will not see us home. C. cannot go away and leave all in new hands. The little Reform Bill for the Government never got through during last session in Parliament. C. wishes to finish that matter off before he goes home, and this he is very decided about. I cannot tell you what a disappointment it was to give up counting the months – now they would have dwindled to six!'

With their departure now postponed until the autumn of the following year Char fell back into 'the usual monotonous life. I repair drawings, read, write and drive. Soon I must make the rounds of the schools. We have had a few of those terrible great dinners which wear me out so, and a great many small ones.' Only the escape to Barrackpore offered solace.

Another member of the Canning circle who had made arrangements to return to England in March 1861, and for whom there was no postponement, was young Johnny Stanley – no longer the foolish boy of whom Lady Canning had once had to write by way of excuse for his behaviour that 'he has no liking for this country & no wonder for he has had a very dull time'. Although not entirely a reformed character, Johnny had at least become a somewhat wiser, less head-

strong individual. He had hated leaving Lady Canning in the hills – writing in his exile from Government House of being 'very wretched in this hot steamy place, do what I will to amuse myself, without Lady Canning' – and had only regained his usual cheerful composure with her return. His last important duty was to attend the Cannings on their second grand tour, this time travelling from Benares into the heart of Central India.

This was a smaller Viceroy's camp than the first and, in Char's opinion, all the better for it – 'This time, I don't know why, I really rather like it.' A long letter written on 23 January from Jubbulpore (Jabalpur, today), some three hundred miles south-west of Benares, gave the Queen a lucid account of some of the tour's main features:

> We left Calcutta late in November & 200 miles of railway took us the same day to the Ganges to join our boat & be towed by a steamer to Benares, the Government Secretaries & their official establishments keeping with us in another 'flat' & steamer – an improvement on the days when Ld Cornwallis or Ld Hastings moved with 300 country boats 'tracked' [towed from the bank] by men. This voyage was even now rather tedious for the low state of the river left little to be seen often for miles together but sandbanks and alligators basking in the sun. There were many places to stop at the [way] – a Durbar was held at Patna for the Bengal Rajahs & Proprietors – many railway works had to be visited, a fine Tunnel at Mongyr & some enormous Bridges in course of building on the artificial foundations of clusters of sunken towers or wells peculiar to India.
>
> In a fortnight we reached the Camp at Benares. We have the smallest possible escort – much smaller than last year's – but still it is like a moving city. The

A lively panorama of the bathing tank at Maihar, visited during the second viceregal tour. New Year's Day, 1861.

Durbar at Benares included the neighbouring Rajahs and some rich merchants, this and Mirzapore being the chief commercial & wealthiest cities of the Bengal Presidency.

At Mirzapore they illuminated the city the day we were encamped there, a sign of good disposition remarkable in these days of taxes which can never be popular, but I believe there is some truth in a story I have heard of the wonder of the natives that if Government wants money why it does not take more!

We missed 3 marches by using the boat as far as Mirzapore and saw the fine old Fort of Chunar where European pensioners are settled. Many are covered with medals & some old soldiers still exist of Ld Lake's time. Ld Canning went to shoot in the preserves of the Benares Rajah. He found it a weary day sitting with the Rajah in a tree – refraining from shooting fine Elks like red deer [Sambhur] in the hope of a tiger who never gave more sign of his presence than by a roar.

From Mirzapore we marched due south rising twice up passes to higher levels of table land. This whole country has had fine crops and provisions were plentiful & cheaper & cheaper every march. We crossed the Rewah territory and were delighted with the whole line of country, which is green & like England & full of many fine trees and running streams. The only traffic along the road which is a good one bordered with trees, seems to be an enormous quantity of cotton in bales on bullocks or in bullock carts – and long streams of pilgrims with earthen jars ornamented with little flags bringing or going to fetch Ganges water. The capital of Rewah is very delapidated and the Rajah is a miserable sufferer from leprosy. He came to meet us in a carriage & was just able to pay a visit. His followers some in armour, others with dresses & horse trappings of gorgeous colour, looked like barbaric figures of very early times.

Jubbulpore where we are at this moment is the extreme point of this march. A great gathering of Rajahs & chiefs have met us here. Holkar from Indore, the Secunder Begum of Bhopal, chiefs from Nagpore, the Pannah Rajah owner of the diamond mines, & many others from far & near. Two Durbars were held to obviate the difficulties on questions of Precedence. Holkar came in great splendour wearing a million's worth of jewels. His show of elephants was very fine. He is a young man & rather of a fanatical turn of mind, everything that was done in [the Maharaja of Gwalior] Scindia's former visits he seems to consider his of rights & due to his dignity. Some details are rather amusing. Scindia gave us an entertainment with fireworks long ago in Calcutta, Holkar was unhappy at not having the same. As an equivalent he decided on requesting us to come to a display of horsemanship & for an hour yesterday we saw a very curious performance by his officers in cloth of gold with their horses covered with gold silver & ribbons prancing about in a most entertaining fashion, varied by Mahratta evolutions of tilting at oranges & firing pistols <u>under</u> their horses.

Much the most interesting person here has been the Begum reigning sovereign of Bhopal. She is a really clever upright character and looks into the affairs of her country herself & rules it admirably. No one disputes her power or her justice.

A photograph of the Maharaja of Indore's elephants at Jubbulpore.

OPPOSITE The redoubtable Begum of Bhopal, wearing the insignia of the newly created Order of the Star of India with which she was invested by Lord Canning at Allahabad in November 1861.

She inherited the country long ago from her Father at the age of 4 years and married her nearest relation. By some strange misapprehension it had been ruled that her daughter 'Shah jehan' shd succeed her on coming of age, but happily the daughter voluntarily gave up all claim during her mother's life & prefers living with her husband 'behind the purdah'. 'Secunder' the reigning Begum is aged 44 and shows her face without compunction, tho' a Mussulman! It is a plain pleasant face with fine intelligent eyes & one longed to hear her talk naturally & without an interpreter. She dislikes all show & parade & wears plain clothes & certainly not becoming ones for her dress is a pair of tight 'kincob' trousers and a small square shawl and a muslin or gauge turban. She & her mother & a female friend or attendant as they sat in the Durbar could hardly be distinguished from little old men.

The Begum Secunder in consideration of her loyalty has been much gratified by receiving a grant of some forfeited territory joining her own. The announcement of this when made to her by Ld Canning at the private Durbar in their first interview quite overcame her. I wished to make some small private present unlike those she wd. receive at the Durbar when I suddenly remembered Nash's

> views of Windsor Castle. It was a happy thought and it was received ardently with great pleasure & the Begum was particularly pleased to see how Your Majesty lived, asking which was the Durbar & which the 'waiting' room.

As well as meeting the local rulers the Cannings were shown the local sights:

> There is here the great establishment for the employment of the Thugs & Robbers whose gangs have been discovered thru' 'approvers' – a whole village exists of the families of these men who are kept under constant supervision. Many are very old & it is one of their arguments to prove that their horrid trade was favoured by Heaven, that they have large thriving families and live to extreme old age. They now are occupied harmlessly in making tents and very good carpets.
>
> This is a lovely country and geologically a very curious one for these are hills of granite and sandstone & marble, and one of the wonders of the world is the channel of the Nerbudda flowing for half a mile between precipices of pure white marble rock, 60 to 120 ft high. Tigers abound in the jungles all along our march in this neighbourhood. Ld Canning hearing of a good chance of one gave himself a holiday & succeeded in shooting a very fine one 9 ft long. It is the 4th killed in the last fortnight by the sportsmen of this camp. The first I saw brought in one evening at dusk made a striking scene, the shooting party returning on a crowd of elephants & the foremost striding along with the great monster across his back. Soon all the camp crowded round as he was examined & measured by torchlight. Panthers seem to do more mischief even than tigers. They go into huts & kill & carry away sleeping men. In this district in the last year 140 tigers were killed & tigers, alone, killed 170 souls! Enormous prices have been set on the heads of the worst offenders, for sometimes the Post is stopped for 2 or 3 days in the hot weather when a 'man eater' occupies the road.

Rounding off her letter with the usual polite enquiries after the various members of the Royal Family, Char added her husband's congratulations on the recent marriage of Princess Alice, signing herself, as always, 'Your Majesty's devoted humble servant, C. Canning'.

Reluctantly leaving her husband to continue his touring in Oude, Char returned to Calcutta on the *Soonamookie* – a frustrating voyage that took three weeks rather than the planned five days as the steamer towing them ran into one sandbank after another: 'At last, on one sandbank we had to leave our steamer altogether, and take another which was free, on the other side of the sand.'

The time had now come for 'little Johnny Stanley' to say his farewells, which he did with very genuine regret: 'As the time to leave this country comes near I feel sorry, I have so many friends somehow whom I feel I like more than ever

OPPOSITE 'One of the wonders of the world'; the narrow cleft through white marble rock cut by the Nerbudda river near Jubbulpore, which Charlotte explored by boat in January 1861.

I fancied & I need hardly say above all these is Lady Canning. Ld C will not break his heart, no more shall I, when we say goodbye, yet I have served him honestly & to the best of my powers although I have never taken to him. I wish he had a firmer mouth, it does so spoil his face.' For Lady Canning, however, Johnny's feelings were very different, as he told his mother with touching candour:

> One never distinctly ascertains how much one values persons & things till on the point of parting with them, & tho' I have always been very fond I did not know what an enormous blank it will make in my insignificant existence not having her to speak to & look at.
>
> When you get this you might write to Lady C (I shall be near home then) & say how much I have worshipped her, for I cannot well say so to her face.

Ten months later Johnny was to send his elder sister Maud a most poignant account of his last meeting with the woman – at forty-four quite old enough to be his mother – whom he so clearly adored:

> The night before I left Calcutta I bought a little gold cross which was made to open & when I went to dear Lady Canning's room to say goodbye to her I asked her (I have often wondered since how I had the courage) if she would put a little bit of hair in it for me to keep as a remembrance of her. I did not wait for her to answer but kissed her hand & ran away. Half an hour after she sent it back with what I had wished for & a few very kind words of parting. I certainly thought then I was the most likely to die first.

Charlotte Canning herself certainly had no such morbid thoughts when she joked in a letter to Lady Sydney in March 1861 that 'by this time next year (if we are alive) we shall be arriving in England'. Even a further six-month postponement of that much desired departure date was accepted without apparent demur: 'C. was pleased with the improvement he found in Oude, which is especially his own work. He is so well, that I do not the least grumble now at the additional year, and feel it would have been very unsatisfactory to have left so much for the smoothing and finishing touches of a successor, after going through all the hardships and most difficult work of the last three years.'

During the Hot Weather of 1861 the Cannings found several opportunities to get away to Barrackpore, frequently in the company of some new friends, Edward and Emily Bayley, to whom they had been introduced by Mrs Bayley's sister, Lady Campbell. In May 1861 Charles Canning offered Mr Bayley the temporary post of Foreign Secretary and invited him and his wife to stay with them for three

months at Government House and Barrackpore. 'In the hot months we went frequently to Barrackpore for short visits', Emily Bayley was to write later:

> It was the only thing in their viceregal life that Lady Canning really cared for. We used to sit in the upper verandah facing the river with a lovely view before us, and the verandah itself full of beautiful flowers brought for her to paint; and, on cooler days, we sat under the great banyan tree in the private garden, reading and working and talking – oh, such happy talks! In the evening, after dinner, we often walked down the long gravel path to watch the stars and revel in the delicious perfume of the flowers. In hot weather, Lady Canning dressed daily in white muslin trimmed with beautiful Valenciennes lace. She always looked charming, but she had no personal vanity whatever.

That summer the Rains came unusually early, making it a 'very bearable year', as far as Char was concerned. Throughout these months every letter carried the same joyful refrain. 'I begin now to believe in going home again', she told her mother in June. 'Now it begins to seem so near.' To her friend Lady Sydney she wrote in July that she could think of 'nothing but the joy of getting home. It seems really near enough now to count the months.' Her only regret was that she would be leaving behind her beloved Barrackpore garden: 'I shall be quite low at parting with that really nice place, and have greatly enjoyed there the command of a tropical garden, where one orders all sorts of hot-house flowers, in groves, and hedges, and thickets. I have literally a double hedge of poinsettia, which will be in a month or two a scarlet wall, and one of dark blue ipomea.' Char's last visit there in September was spent tidying up her drawings and paintings. To a favourite aunt, the Dowager Countess of Caledon, she wrote:

> I have been very busy over my scrap-books of sketches, and writing, or causing to be written, the names etc, and it is all rather tidily done now – two volumes and a portfolio full, a few more flowers and a great bundle of journal of the last march. In course of time, if you are at very complete leisure, you may not think it duller than Mrs Anybody's travels from a book-club.

In the same letter Char could also write that she looked upon the 'hard trial of India' as almost over. She had only one more week of Calcutta's heat and humidity to endure, 'for next Monday I go off with my maid and two captains to Darjeeling. I hope it does not shock you to think of such independence, but I am very old now, and can go anywhere with anybody.'

A visit to Darjeeling had been a long-cherished ambition of Lady Canning's and, in what was to be her last letter to the Queen, written on 15 September, she gave details of what was planned to be her final adventure in India before returning home:

> I am about to make another little tour to the hills & to see Darjeeling which ought to be the Sanatorium of Calcutta – as it is but 350 miles off – but it is still a tedious journey after crossing the Ganges and above 200 miles of railway there is still at least 3 nights travelling in the most disagreeable of all conveyances – a palanquin!
>
> I look forward with much pleasure to this excursion for I have sometimes felt rather worn out after so much heat and I am going to a spot with the highest mountains in the world immediately before one in full view. Ld Canning is unable to give himself this real treat & I am to hurry back to join him at Allahabad for the Investitures on the 1st of November which I would not miss on any account.

The Allahabad investiture concerned the new Indian order of chivalry of the Star of India, created at Lord Palmerston's advice and suggestion – and with the Queen's enthusiastic support – as part of his general policy of putting Indians as far as possible on the same footing as Britons in India. Although half a dozen loyal Indian princes headed the first complement of names, the first knight to be invested was Lord Clyde's successor as Commander in Chief, Sir Hugh Rose, who was given his own ceremony in Calcutta prior to Char's departure for Darjeeling:

> The sight was really a fine one, for owing to opening out an area to throw two Halls together a great number of persons could be assembled & Ld Canning stood in front of the Throne to invest the Commander in Chief. The very beautiful design of the jewel was admired by every one, and also the very magnificent collar, but I am afraid it will be found that the native Knights will not be inclined to understand however much it is explained that they are not personal property but have to be returned by their heirs.

The ceremony was followed in the evening by a large dinner for eighty and a party 'to which all the principal natives came, as well as the whole of English society, and Armenians, Greeks, etc, settled here'. Lady Canning was reported to have been unusually radiant and lively that evening and full of her usual grace and charm, dressed in white satin and wearing a diamond coronet, with a long sprig of ivy entwined in her dark hair. This was her last public appearance in Calcutta and one long remembered.

Charlotte arrived in Darjeeling on 7 October, riding up the last stretch of moun-

OPPOSITE The last photograph, probably taken at Barrackpore in the autumn of 1861, showing all too clearly the changes wrought by nearly six years of living in India.

tain track on her white pony. Apart from the occasional 'dazzle of a headache', she arrived apparently none the worse for her journey through the notorious *terai* jungle that guarded the approach to the Himalayas – notorious on account of the supposed 'poisonous emanations' produced in its dense forests that were believed to cause the most severe form of ague known as remittent fever. The dense jungles and 'clothed hills' delighted Char: 'The forests never cease & give me an idea of damp as I never saw, but then it is such wonderful luxuriance – quite unlike all else tho' perhaps I saw forests as fine before, yet never anything like this extent of them – it is as if the whole country round Simla was clothed with enormous trees & creepers & underwood, & tied together with cables of creeper, not much in flower now.'

This last quotation is from one of a number of letters sent from Darjeeling to Charles Canning in Allahabad – the only ones written to him from Char that are known to have survived. All are shot through with her love and devotion for her husband, her 'Darling Carlo', but they also show her to have been much preoccupied with plans for the future. From time to time brief accounts of her surroundings – of excursions at dawn to see the sun's rays strike Mount Everest or of expeditions further afield to the frontiers of Sikkim – are included but it is obvious that the writer's heart is elsewhere.

Of the scores of letters written to his wife by Lord Canning – and he is said to have written to her daily while he was in Allahabad and she in Darjeeling – only a single example survives. Written two years earlier, while she was on her Himalayan trek and he in Calcutta, it suggests in the affectionate, good-humoured intimacy of its tone that there was some truth in Minny Stuart's later assertion, seconded by Mrs Bayley, that she had 'much reason to think that the last two years had been happier to both than they had known for many, many past ones', years in which Char found 'almost a reminiscence of the perfect happiness of her married life'. The warm closing lines in Charles Canning's Calcutta letter – 'Goodbye, my own darling Char. It is a great comfort to know that tim [apparently Lord Canning's pet name for his wife] is really enjoying itself. Blessings on it. Your own C.' – are not those of an estranged husband. And Char's letters from Darjeeling all end in the same deeply affectionate vein: 'I have your very darling letter. Goodbye Treasure. Your own Char'.

When Char heard from her husband in Allahabad that the Queen had offered him the honorary office of the Rangership of Blackheath, and with it the elegant Ranger's House on the edge of Greenwich Park, her happiness knew no bounds. She at once set to work speculating and planning and dreaming:

> I like it very much indeed – almost better than the old Lodge. It is not so pretty

but I think there is more ground and in every way it will be very nice to have. One can have plenty of plants & potager & laundry, & the old part & common are charming – there is no sort of view but one can make it nice, & it will answer so well to store away things & one can have charming dinners of friends & fresh whitebait for them. I like it so very much, & a garden for plenty of flowers one can have there as well as anywhere else & perhaps a farm too & at least a poultry yard & cows for we can surely turn them out in Greenwich park. It is such a very new idea. Stuffed birds, curiosities, all sorts of rubbish can go there and be quite a resource. I only remember of garden a green paddock with a shrubbery single walk all round, but of course that could be made available for flowers & fruit & there may be a kitchen garden.

I am afraid you have not written for ages to the Queen, it is very nice of her to do you this little personal civility herself & so graciously.

Goodbye darling,
Your own Char.

Besides these visions of future domesticity – 'Every hour I remember something which makes it more convenient . . . I am so fond of my Blackheath Villa in my mind's eye . . . We must have some Cochin fowls . . . the dairy I specially like the thought of' – more disturbing hints are contained in these letters of increasing ill health, of 'interior derangement' and feverish, sleepless nights. 'My grievance is still not sleeping', runs one such comment. 'I have often slept badly but never as badly as now & I do not know now when I shall ever sleep again.' When news came from Allahabad that she was not to join Charles for the investiture, there was as much relief as disappointment in her answer:

Darling Carlo.

I have just got your letter about the Allahabad journey & now I feel really very much ashamed of being so poor spirited, & of being away from my post after always following like the faithful little dog. I think it really looks as if it would be rather a relief to you that I did not come. It is even now pouring with rain & on such a day as this I could not get away. Then as to this place doing me good in health, I don't think it does, for I sleep shockingly, but then again I have a little bowel disarrangement, and tho' I am sure I could have got thro' it all quite well, I believe it is wiser to give it up.

Lady Canning left Darjeeling early on the morning of Monday 4 November, being escorted down from the mountains by the Secretary of the Governor of Bengal, Major Pugh. 'I rode part of the way down the hill with her', he later recorded. 'She talked constantly of her return to England, of a house which the Queen had kindly placed at her disposal, and of interesting things she had collected to take home, and she invited us to visit her and see them. On reaching the plains, ignorant

of the risk she ran, as the ground was not yet thoroughly dry, she ordered the palanquin to be set down in the fog, while she took one last sketch of the distant mountains.'

Charlotte was almost certainly already in the grip of intermittent fever long before she began her return journey through the *terai*. The rigours of travelling merely helped to exacerbate her already weakened condition.

She arrived in Calcutta in a state of collapse, the shocked Commander of the Viceroy's Bodyguard sent to meet her at once diagnosing 'Purnea fever' – that being the name of the little civil station on the edge of the *terai* through which Char had passed.

Char rallied sufficiently to be able to write a few letters, among them a brief note to her friend Mrs Bayley, whose advanced pregnancy had prevented her from joining Char in Darjeeling and who was now confined to her house in Calcutta. She apologised for being unable to call, she had caught 'a little of the Purneah fever' and as a result of the 'almost incessant running [of the palanquin] from Monday very early day & night' was 'pretty knocked up'. To her husband, now on his way back from Allahabad, she wrote to say that she was safe at her journey's end but 'so very very shaken & tired. I think I ache more than I ought & shall treat it as fever & take a calomel & opium pill & be quite well before you come'. Yet even in her feverish state Char could not quite forget her hopes: 'We must get bamboo milk pails in Burmah for I have only one & I believe they are bigger there. Goodbye treasure, Your own Char.'

Charles Canning, accompanied by Dr Beale, arrived in Calcutta on 10 November to find Char 'complaining a little of headache & fatigue, and a little feverish' but well enough to show him her latest drawings 'with all her usual interest'. For two days she remained weak and 'indisposed to much exertion' but appeared to be getting no worse. Then her condition deteriorated so suddenly that her husband and friends at Government House could do no more than watch and pray. With meticulous and characteristic reserve, Charles Canning wrote – for his Sovereign – an account of this unremitting decline into death:

> This was Tuesday the 12th, and from that day the fever increased strongly. It was plain that it had laid strong hold of the system. It was continuous – not intermittent – and therefore the more weakening, and more difficult to deal with. There was not much restlessness and not much acute pain; only a general aching of the limbs. She was perfectly conscious and able to talk (though not much disposed to do so) till Thursday. On that day the mind began to wander, but only occasionally. On Friday the bad symptoms increased, whilst the fever had scarcely abated for an hour. The doctors declared that it would be a struggle of strength

> between the disease and the constitution and this was too evidently the truth. On Saturday morning however the fever did abate. The good symptoms continued throughout that day and part of the night, and Lord Canning was full of hope. Even the Doctors, both of whom had great experience of these fevers, said that it was a very positive and decided improvement.
>
> But early on Sunday morning the disease returned – more terribly than ever. What little strength had been regained was soon lost. The pulse, which had come down to 100, rose again to 130. Weakness increased visibly, in spite of constant stimulants & strengthening food, and there was more restlessness and quickness of breathing. This state of things continued through Sunday until about midnight. Then the breathing became easier, but the pulse more & more weak. At ½ past 2 o'clock on Monday morning she died quite calmly in Lord Canning's arms. There was never any pain – probably, at last, no consciousness – but the same gentle, patient, unrepining look which from the beginning had never left her face for an instant.

For the last four days and nights of her illness Lord Canning had scarcely left his wife's side, allowing no one other than the doctors and nurses attending her to enter the room. After her death he emerged, by every account, a broken man, never to recover his health. As custom demanded in India, the funeral took place on the day after Lady Canning's death, at sunrise on 19 November. The site that Lord Canning chose for her grave was a fitting one: a corner of what Char had always thought of as *her* garden at Barrackpore: 'It is a beautiful spot – looking upon that reach of the grand river which she was so fond of drawing, shaded from the glare of the sun by high trees, and amongst the bright shrubs and flowers in which she had so much pleasure.'

The interment at Barrackpore; the scene at the graveside on the morning of 19 November 1861, recorded by a friend in the Public Works Department, Charles D'Oyly, who had spent that night supervising the building of a vault.

L. B. Bowring, who had been Lord Canning's Private Secretary since 1858, was among the little group, made up almost entirely of the Viceroy's staff officers, which attended the interment. He, the four ADCs and the Commander of the Bodyguard, acted as pallbearers. Many years later he set down his account of Lady Canning's last journey to her resting place:

> In the dead of the next night a solemn procession passed slowly over the great ballroom at the top of Government House, down the broad staircase and the splendid flight of steps at the main entrance, and deposited its solemn burden in a gun-carriage drawn by eight horses. The staff followed in the viceregal carriages and the funeral cortege proceeded at a slow pace to Barrackpore, where it arrived at sunrise, Lord Canning having gone on before. As the first rays of the sun lit up the Ganges, the sad group, with the Viceroy at their head, accompanied the coffin to a grassy knoll in the private garden, visible from the river, but hidden from the public park, and here we laid the mortal part of the gifted and beautiful Countess Canning. We sorrowed greatly for her husband as we thought of the contrast between the close of the eventful administration, pregnant with startling incidents, but crowned with ultimate success, and the desolation which had fallen upon his private life.
>
> Gossip-mongers were not wanting who averred that there was an estrangement between husband and wife, but all I can say is that I never perceived it, for although Lord Canning, under the pressure of business, kept much to his own room, where he generally breakfasted and lunched alone, he was invariably most considerate towards her, showing her every mark of attention, while his behaviour on her death proved how truly he loved and esteemed her.

Char's flower-strewn grave beside the waters of the Hooghly.

EPILOGUE

By sad coincidence the death of the Viceroy's consort in India was followed in England a month later by the death of the Prince Consort, the telegram announcing Lady Canning's demise reaching the Queen just nine days before the death of Prince Albert. Nearly a month passed before the Queen was able to write to Lord Canning but her letter, as unrestrained in its outpouring of grief as Canning had been reticent in his, spoke most powerfully and movingly of their shared loss:

> Osborne
> January 10th 1862
>
> Lord Canning little thought when he wrote his kind and touching letter of the 22nd November, that it would only reach the Queen when she was smitten and bowed down to the earth by an event similar to the one which he describes – and, strange to say, by a disease greatly analogous to the one which took from him all that he loved best. In the case of her adored, precious, perfect, and great husband, her dear lord and master, to whom this Nation owed more than it can ever truly know, however, the fever went on most favourably till the day previous to the awful calamity.
>
> To lose one's partner in life is, as Lord Canning knows, like losing half of one's body and soul, torn forcibly away – and dear Lady Canning was such a dear, worthy devoted wife! But to the Queen – to a poor helpless woman – it is like death in life! Great and small – nothing was done without his loving advice and help – and she feels alone in the wide world, with many helpless children to look to her – and the whole nation to look to her – now when she can barely struggle with her wretched existence! Her misery – her utter despair – she cannot describe! Her only support – the only ray of comfort she gets for a moment, is in the firm conviction and certainty of his nearness, his undying love, and of their eternal reunion! Only she prays always, and pines for the latter with an anxiety she cannot describe. Like dear Lady Canning, the Queen's darling is to rest in a garden – at Frogmore.
>
> May God comfort and support Lord Canning, and may he think in his sorrow of his widowed and broken-hearted Sovereign – bowed to the earth with the greatest of human sufferings and misfortunes.

Although perhaps for different reasons, Lord Canning's loss left him equally bereft. In a memorial album of photographs and letters dedicated to the 'cherished

memory of my dearly loved friend', Emily Bayley (who had been delivered of a baby girl, Charlotte Canning Bayley, on the very morning of Lady Canning's death) wrote of Charles Canning:

> Poor Lord Canning became an old decrepid man from the day of her death, walking with a stick and an ADC's arm to support him. He visited the grave every night after dark – a lamp was kept burning there. Then when he began to overlook her papers, letters and diaries he started to break down altogether. He then realized for the first time how deeply she had suffered for some years and how devoted, self-sacrificing and loyal had been her love for him all her life! It was too late then to make amends to her – but remorse broke down his health and he mourned for her in truest deepest love & reverence – anguish for her loss really killed him.

Even if Mrs Bayley's sense of loyalty may have led her to draw exaggerated conclusions, there can be no doubt that Lord Canning's reactions to his wife's death were enough to alarm his friends. Major Bowie, now his Military Secretary, observed him in lonely vigil at the graveside at four in the morning on Christmas Day 1861, and however late his work kept him in Calcutta on Saturday evening nothing could stop him from driving out to Barrackpore that same evening to place fresh flowers on her grave.

A marble cross and tomb, designed by Louisa Waterford, was later placed over the grave, bearing an inscription that Lord Canning himself had written shortly after Char's death:

> Honours and praises written on a tomb are at best but vain-glory; but that her charity, humility, meekness and watchful faith in her Saviour will, for that Saviour's sake, be accepted of God, and be to her a glory everlasting, is the firm trust of those who knew her best, and most dearly loved her in life, and who cherish the memory of her, departed.

Wishing to establish a more practical memorial, a committee of Calcutta ladies came up with a proposal that was very much in accordance with Lady Canning's own wishes. From funds raised by public subscription a hostel was established in Calcutta for European nurses.

On 12 March 1862 Lord Elgin arrived in Calcutta to take over the reins of office from his predecessor. As the two met observers were struck by the contrast between the new Viceroy, who 'came up gaily, ruddy in face, buoyant in manner, and stalwart in frame', and the old – 'pale, wan, toilworn and grief-stricken'. After

OPPOSITE Earl Canning, KC, photographed just before his departure from India, barely four months after Char's death and three months before his own.

spending the afternoon at Barrackpore by his wife's grave, Canning sailed down-river after dark in the steamship *Feroze* on 18 March, his six-year tenure of office completed. In his assessment of these hard years, Lord Elgin concluded that Charles Canning's greatest achievement had been his policy of reconciliation between Government and all sections of British and Indian society, a policy adhered to in the face of the bitterest opposition but which had ultimately 'opened up a new future for India'. The epithet of 'Clemency', bestowed on him in anger, was to become a badge of honour, adding lustre to a reputation – rare among India's pro-consuls – that both Indians and Britons equally could respect.

Now in Canada on active service with the Coldstream Guards, Johnny Stanley received a full account of Lady Canning's death and interment from Major Bowie. Writing to his sister, he told her how sad it was to get his letters returned unopened from Calcutta: 'In reading through there is so much I had not said before & should have liked her to know. It is not easy nor necessary even to say much on such a subject & the more deeply one feels the less natural it is to write about it. I still, when in my room, think as much as ever.' Johnny afterwards married a Miss Susan Mackenzie.

Arriving in England on 26 April, Lord Canning went immediately to Highcliffe Castle to pay his respects to Lady Stuart de Rothesay and Char's sister, Lady Waterford. It was a painful visit for all concerned, made no easier by Charles Canning's unwillingness to talk about the past. After a few days he moved on to visit Charles and Minny Stuart in their Hampshire home. 'There is not much to tell of Lord Canning's visit', wrote Mrs Stuart to their old friends in India, Sir Edward and Lady Campbell:

> The grand, pale sad face came here – and met us all – with evident suffering but wondrous self-restraint!! I wish he had seen you two for when he finally met me and I spoke he shook from head to foot and the very flesh on his face quivered! But he said nothing – not even alluded to the past. He would feel still more strongly your more recent association with that blessed and now happy creature. I feel that he will never speak of the past. Twice friends tried to speak of her, and he burst into tears and could not do it.

Lord Canning was next expected to call upon the Queen but it seems that both Sovereign and subject were anxious to avoid meeting for the time being – 'She dreaded it, poor thing, for herself and for him', wrote Mrs Stuart. Returning, instead, to his town house in Grosvenor Square on 5 May, Charles at once fell seriously ill. According to L. B. Bowring, 'alarming symptoms' in the form of acute inflammation of the liver and diarrhoea soon became apparent:

> On sending for his old Indian medical adviser, Dr Beale, that gentleman at once perceived that his end was nigh, and told Lady Clanricarde, his sister that he should be warned that he had only a few days to live. On this alarming intelligence being conveyed to him, he merely said, 'What! So soon!', and prepared himself for death. Many of his old friends came to see him as life was waning, and the regard and affection which they evinced towards him proved how much he was esteemed by them.

Shortly before the moment of death Charles Canning was told by his sister that he was 'going to Char', at which 'his whole countenance' was said to have 'brightened up'. He died on 17 June and was buried four days later in Westminster Abbey, his old friend Lord Clyde supporting another, Sir James Outram, as they followed his coffin up the aisle. Lady Stuart de Rothesay, on hearing of his death, is reported to have thrown up her hands and exclaimed, with tears streaming down her face, 'Here *is* judgement!'

In Calcutta an equestrian statue of the first Viceroy was erected outside Government House. A century later it was removed by order of a newly elected Marxist Government of Bengal – only to be re-erected by some generous spirit within the enclosure that surrounds Lady Canning's tomb at Barrackpore. The Viceroy's country seat now serves as a police hospital, while Barrackpore park belongs to the Military Police and is much built over. But three hundred yards south of the main house Charlotte Canning's grave lies secluded and undisturbed, guarded at the head by the spreading branches of a tamarind tree, at the foot by the statue of her husband, who looks down upon her tomb and beyond towards the broad sweep of the Hooghly.

Most curiously, Lady Canning's name lives on in Bengal in the shape of an Indian sweetmeat known as *ledikeni*, a ball of flour, sugar and curd deep fried in syrup to which she was supposed to have been rather partial. It is a strange little accident of history that Char would have found highly amusing.

Three years after Char's death a monument of white marble, executed by Sir Gilbert Scott to a design by her sister, Louise, was erected over her grave.

SOURCES

Abbreviations: RA Royal Archives, IOLR Indian Office Library & Records, CP Canning Papers (Leeds District Archives)

Introduction: 'A Cloud May Arise'

PAGE

3 For a full account of Lady Canning's early years and her term as Lady of the Bedchamber see *Charlotte Canning* by Virginia Surtees, (John Murray, 1975).

4 The Private Secretary was L. B. Bowring, appointed in Jan. 1858, whose journals are preserved in the IOLR (MSS. EUR. G.91).

4 James Bruce (1811–63), 8th Earl of Elgin & 12th of Kincardine, was Governor of Jamaica 1842, Gov.-Gen. of Canada 1846–54, Envoy to China 1857–8 & 1860–1, Viceroy of India 1862–3. His remarks were made to Lady Bayley (wife of Sir Edward Bayley, Foreign Secy & Home Secy under Lord Canning 1861–2), who compiled a memorial album of letters, photographs and personal reminiscences after Lady Canning's death (IOLR MSS. EUR. D.661).

4 Queen Victoria's letter to Lady Canning of 28 May 1842 is quoted by kind permission of Lord Harewood and is among Lady Canning's letters and journals preserved in Leed's District Archives (CP).

7 & 9 The extracts from Queen Victoria's journal are quoted by gracious permission of Her Majesty the Queen (RA *Queen Victoria's Journal* Dec. 20 1842 & Nov. 22 1855).

7 & 8 Lady Canning's letters to her mother, Lady Stuart de Rothesay, and to her sister Louisa, the Marchioness of Waterford, are quoted from *The Story of Two Noble Lives*, Vols I & II, by Augustus Hare, George Allen, 1893.

8 Queen Victoria's letter to R. V. Smith, President of the Board of Control, is quoted from *Letters of Queen Victoria 1837–61*, Vol.III, by A. C. Benson & Lord Esher, 1907.

8 An example of this gossip can be found in the journals of F. W. H. Cavendish, published as *Society, Politics and Diplomacy*, 1913.

9 Lord Canning's speech is given in full in *Earl Canning* by Sir H. P. Cunningham, 1891.

Chapter One: 'How Like a Dream'

10 For accounts of the overland journey see Emma Roberts, *Overland Journey to Bombay*, 1845, and J. H. Stocquelier, *Handbook of British India*, 1854. The steamship service between Bombay and Suez commenced in 1830, the first Indian mail reaching England in fifty-nine days. By 1843 Bombay had been brought within thirty days of London and two years later a fortnightly mail service was introduced. Lady Canning's journal-letters were therefore written over a two-week period, with a fair copy being sent with the mail steamer as a letter.

10, 11, 12 & 13 Lady Canning to Queen Victoria, Cairo Dec. 19 1855 (RA Z 502/1).

14, 16, 19 & 21 Lady Canning to Queen Victoria, Madras Feb. 24 1856 (RA Z 502/2). Extracts from Lady Canning's journal-letters and letters (CP) quoted in this and in subsequent chapters and mostly quoted direct from Hare (*opus cit.*) Vols II & III.

21 Queen Victoria to Lady Canning, Windsor Castle Jan. 25 1856 (CP).

Chapter Two: 'I Never Knew What Idleness Was Before'

23 Lady Canning to Queen Victoria, Calcutta Mar. 8 1856 (RA Z 502/3).

26 Lady Canning to Queen Victoria, Calcutta Aug. 8 1856 (RA Z 502/4).

23 For accounts of Lord Dalhousie's Governor-Generalship and health see Lord Curzon's *British Government in India*, Vol.I, Cassell, 1925.

24 For details of Government House, Calcutta see Curzon (*op. cit.*) Vol.II.

33 Lord Dunkellin's letters are quoted from Michael Maclagan's monumental study of Charles Canning, *'Clemency' Canning*, Macmillan, 1962. (See also British Museum ADD. MSS. 47469.)

Chapter Three: 'A Different Stage of Existence'

37 Queen Victoria to Lady Canning, Buckingham Palace June 22 1856 (CP).

38, 39, 40 & 41 Lady Canning to Queen Victoria, Barrackpore Oct. 7 (RA Z 502/5).

39 For details of Government House, Barrackpore see Curzon (*op. cit.*) Vol.II.

41 For accounts of the Bengal Army and the disposition of troops see Philip Mason's *A Matter of Honour*, Jonathan Cape, 1974.

43 Queen Victoria to Lady Canning, Balmoral Sep. 23 1856 (CP).

48 Lady Canning to Queen Victoria, Barrackpore Nov. 23 (1856) (RA Z 502/6).

48 & 49 Lady Canning to Queen Victoria,

Calcutta Jan. 8 1857 (RA Z 502/7).
49 Lady Canning to Queen Victoria, Calcutta Feb. 23 1857 (RA Z 502/8).

Chapter Four: 'Burning and Murdering and Horrors'

51 For the most objective accounts of the events of 1857 see Christopher Hibbert's *The Great Mutiny: India 1857*, Allen Lane, 1978 and *The Indian Mutiny of 1857* by Surendra Nath Sen, Delhi, 1958. See also Maclagan, (*op. cit.*). For a personal account of events see Vol.I of *Forty-One Years in India* by Field Marshal Lord Roberts, VC, 1897.
51 & 56 Lady Canning to Queen Victoria, Calcutta May 19 1857 (RA Z 502/10).
52 Lady Canning to Queen Victoria, Calcutta Apr. 9 1857 (RA Z 502/9).
52 & 53 Queen Victoria to Lady Canning, Buckingham Palace July 5 1857 (CP).
57 Bowring journal (IOLR MSS. EUR. G.91).
58 General Anson was only sixty at the outbreak of the Mutiny, a stripling compared to other Indian Army commanders. Sir Henry Havelock was sixty-two; Sir John Hearsey sixty-four; Sir Colin Campbell (Lord Clyde) sixty-five; General W. H. 'Bloody Bill' Hewitt (Commander of the Meerut Division) sixty-seven; Sir Hugh Wheeler (Commander of the Cawnpore Garrison) was sixty-nine; Sir Mark Cubbon (v. Chapter Seven) seventy-two.
60 The Queen's Birthday was, of course, 24 May but 24 May in 1857 was a Sunday which is presumably why it was celebrated on 25 May.
61, 62 & 64 Lady Canning to Queen Victoria, Calcutta June 5 1857 (RA Z 502/11).

Chapter Five: 'Remember Cawnpore'

68 For a contemporary account of the Cawnpore tragedy see George Trevelyan's *Cawnpore*, 1865. A full list of personal narratives of the Mutiny is given in Hibbert (*op. cit.*).
70 & 71 Lady Canning to Queen Victoria, Calcutta July 20 1857 (RA Z 502/13).
71 & 73 Lady Canning to Queen Victoria, Calcutta Aug. 10 1857 (RA Z 502/14).
74, 76 & 78 Lady Canning to Queen Victoria, Calcutta Sep. 10 1857 (RA Z 502/17).
77 Lord Canning to Queen Victoria, Calcutta Sep. 25 1857 (RA N 15/89).
77 Lord Canning's 'Clemency' Resolution is given in full in Maclagan (*op. cit.*), Appendix II.
78 & 79 Queen Victoria to Lady Canning, Balmoral Castle Sep. 8 1857 (CP).
80 Lady Canning to Queen Victoria, Calcutta Oct. 23 1857 (RA Z 502/21).
80 & 81 Queen Victoria to Lady Canning, Windsor Castle Oct. 22 1857 (CP).

Chapter Six: 'Lucknow is Saved'

82 & 85 Lady Canning to Queen Victoria, Calcutta Nov. 10 1857 (RA Z 502/23).
86 Lady Canning to Queen Victoria, Calcutta Oct. 23 1857 (RA Z 502/21).
86 Queen Victoria to Lady Canning, Windsor Castle Dec. 24 1857 (CP).
91 & 92 Lady Canning to Queen Victoria, Calcutta Nov. 25 1857 (RA Z 502/24).
89 Lady Canning to Queen Victoria, Calcutta Feb. 9 1858 (RA Z 502/33).
88, 91 & 92 Lady Canning to Queen Victoria, Calcutta Jan. 9 1858 (RA Z 502/30).
93 & 94 Excerpts from the Stuarts' letters are taken from Hare (*op. cit.*) Vol.II.

Chapter Seven: 'A Glimpse of the Burning Plain'

96 Lady Canning to Queen Victoria, Barrackpore Feb. 9 1858 (RA Z 502/33).
96 Lady Canning to Queen Victoria, Calcutta Feb. 23 1858 (RA Z 502/34).
96 Queen Victoria to Lady Canning, Buckingham Palace Feb. 8 1858 (CP).
97 Johnny Stanley's letters are quoted by kind permission of Lord Stanley of Alderley. More about him and his most interesting family may be found in *The Stanleys of Alderley*, edited by Nancy Mitford, Hamish Hamilton, 1939.
98 Lady Canning to Queen Victoria, Guindy nr Madras Mar. 14 1858 (RA Z 502/35).
98 Lady Canning to Queen Victoria, Nandydroog nr Bangalore Mar. 24 1858 (RA A 502/38).
99 Lady Canning to Queen Victoria, Coonoor Nilgherry Hills Apr. 8 1858 (RA Z 502/41).
104 Lady Canning to Queen Victoria, Coonoor Nilgherry Hills May 18 1858 (RA Z 502/46).
105 Lord Ellenborough's outburst is given in full in Maclagan (*op. cit.*).
106 Lady Canning to Lady Sydney, see Hare (*op. cit.*) Vol.II.
107 Queen Victoria to Lady Canning, Buckingham Palace July 1 1858 (CP)
107 & 108 Mrs Stuart to Lady Stuart de Rothesay, see Hare (*op. cit.*) Vol.II.

Chapter Eight: 'A New Order of Things'

109 & 110 Lady Canning to Queen Victoria, Allahabad Aug. 30 1858 (RA Z 502/50).
115 The Queen's Proclamation is given in full in Maclagan (*op. cit.*), Appendix IV. For a contrary view see W. H. Russell's *My Diary in India*, 1860.
115 Lady Canning to Queen Victoria, Allahabad Nov. 2 1858 (RA Z 502/51).
116 Lady Canning to Queen Victoria, Allahabad Dec. 13 1858 (RA Z 502/52).
116 Lady Canning to Queen Victoria,

Allahabad Jan. 15 1859 (RA Z 502/53).

116 & 117 Lady Canning to Queen Victoria, Calcutta Feb. 9 1859 (RA Z 502/54).

118 & 120 Lady Canning to Queen Victoria, Barrackpore Aug. 22 1859 (RA Z 502/62).

121, 122 & 123 Lady Canning to Queen Victoria, Camp Cawnpore Nov. 2 1859 (RA Z 502/63).

123 Queen Victoria to Lady Canning, Osborne Dec. 9 1859 (CP).

Chapter Nine: 'A Wild Journey'

125 Field Marshal Lord Roberts (*op. cit.*) Vol.I.

126 & 127 Lady Canning to Queen Victoria, Governor-General's Camp, Umballa Jan. 17 1860 (RA Z 502/64).

132 & 135 Lady Canning to Queen Victoria, Simla Apr. 20 1860 (RA Z 502/65).

135 Queen Victoria to Lady Canning, Windsor Castle Feb. 17 1860 (CP).

139, 140, 141, 142 & 143 Lady Canning to Queen Victoria, Landour near Mussoorie June 28 1860 (RA Z 502/66).

143 Queen Victoria to Lady Canning, Windsor Castle Dec. 17 1860 (CP).

Chapter Ten: 'The Hard Trial of India'

146 Lady Canning to Queen Victoria, Government House, Calcutta Aug. 9 1860 (RA Z 502/67).

148, 149, 151 & 152 Lady Canning to Queen Victoria, Camp Jubbulpore Jan. 23 1861 (RA Z 502/68).

152 Lady Canning's mention of 'the recent marriage of Princess Alice' referred to the Princess's engagement to Prince Loun of Hesse which was announced in December 1860. They were not married until July 1862.

155 Lady Bayley's thoughts were set down in her memorial volume (IOLR MSS. EUR. D.661).

155 Lady Canning's letter to Lady Caledon, see Hare (*op. cit.*) Vol.III.

156 Lady Canning to Queen Victoria, Calcutta Sep. 15 1861 (RA Z 502/69).

158 Lady Canning's surviving letters to Lord Canning and his single letter to her are in the Leeds District Archives (CP).

158 Mrs Stuart's letter is preserved in Lady Bayley's memorial volume (IOLR MSS EUR. D.661).

160 & 161 Lord Canning to Queen Victoria, Barrackpore Nov. 22 1861 (RA N 26/6).

162 Bowring journals (IOLR MSS. EUR. G.911).

Epilogue

163 Queen Victoria to Lord Canning quoted by Benson & Esher (*op. cit.*) Vol.III.

165 Lady Bayley's memorial volume (IOLR MSS. EUR. D.661).

165 The striking difference between the two viceroys was noted by Sir Richard Temple and recorded in *Men and Events of My Time in India*, 1882.

166 Mrs Stuart's letters, see Lady Bayley's memorial volume (IOLR MSS. EUR. D.661).

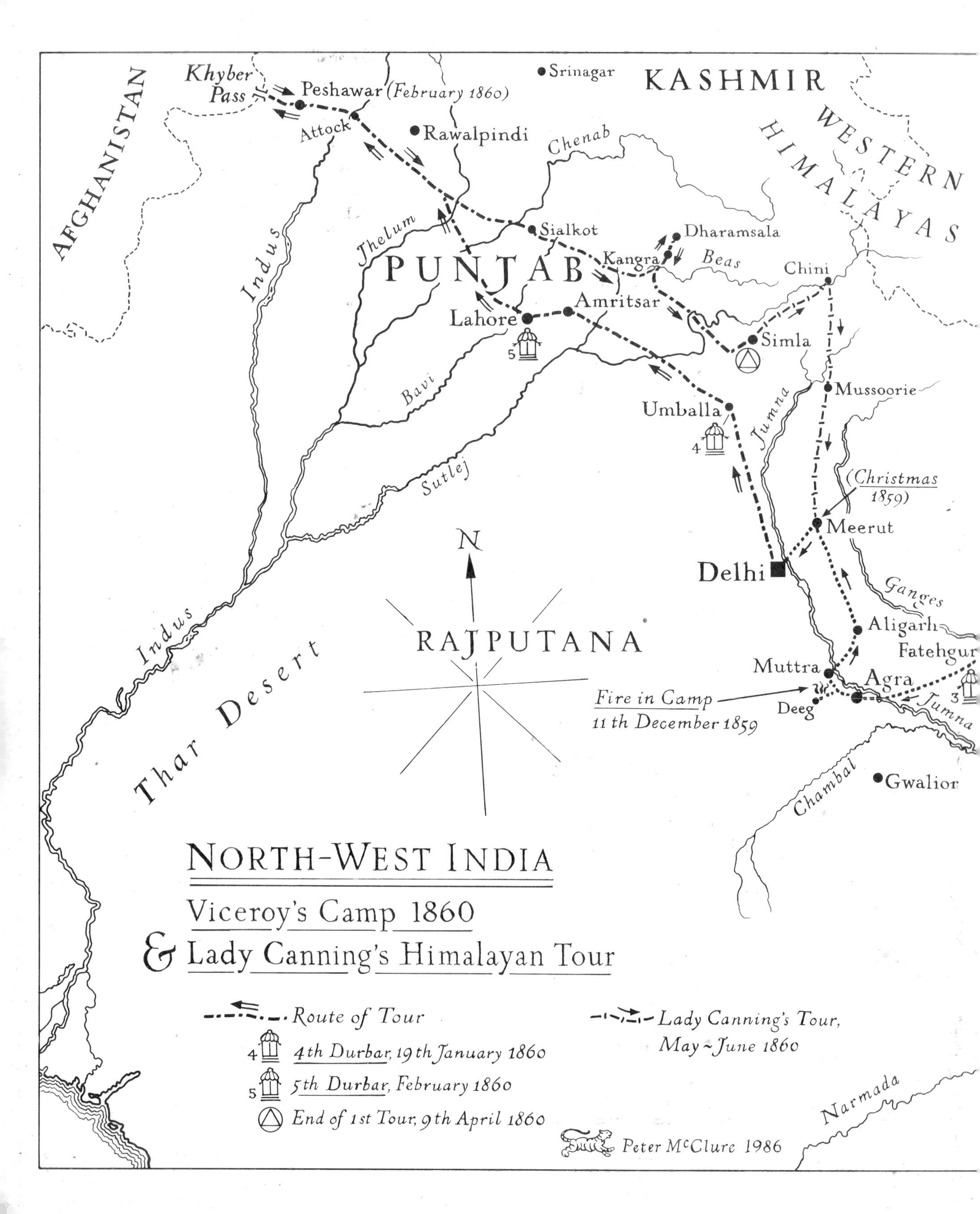

NORTH-WEST INDIA
Viceroy's Camp 1860
& Lady Canning's Himalayan Tour
Route of Tour
4th Durbar, 19th January 1860
5th Durbar, February 1860
End of 1st Tour, 9th April 1860
Lady Canning's Tour, May–June 1860
Peter McClure 1986
AFGHANISTAN
Khyber Pass
Peshawar (February 1860)
Attock
Rawalpindi
Srinagar
KASHMIR
WESTERN HIMALAYAS
Chenab
Jhelum
Indus
PUNJAB
Sialkot
Dharamsala
Kangra
Beas
Chini
Lahore
Amritsar
Simla
Bavi
Sutlej
Umballa
Jumna
Mussoorie
(Christmas 1859)
Meerut
Delhi
Ganges
Aligarh
Fatehgur
Muttra
Agra
Fire in Camp
11th December 1859
Deeg
Chambal
Gwalior
RAJPUTANA
N
Thar Desert
Narmada